He opened his ▮▮▮▮▮ **hers, licking the** ▮▮▮▮▮ **lips from end to end, tugging on them gently before pulling away.**

Her panting breaths mingled with his and he groaned huskily as he spoke against her mouth.

"If we don't stop now, Emma, I don't think I can. And as much as I want to pick you up and do all kinds of carnal things to this sexy body of yours—" he stopped, drawing in a deep breath "—I don't want you to think I'm trying to manipulate you, trying to…" He closed his eyes. "I just don't want to screw this up. I—"

When she placed a hand over his lips, his eyes opened to see her staring up at him.

"You're not manipulating me. I know exactly what I'm doing. I know exactly what I want."

He drew in a harsh breath when her small hand reached between them to stroke the front of his pants, cupping his bulge through the thick fabric of his jeans.

"And what I want is you. Now."

Books by Kimberly Kaye Terry

Kimani Romance

Hot to Touch

KIMBERLY KAYE TERRY

Kimberly Kaye Terry's love for reading romances began at an early age. Long into the night she would stay up until she reached "The End" with her Mickey Mouse night-light on, praying she wouldn't be caught reading what her mother called *those* types of books. Often, she would acquire her stash of *those* books from beneath her mother's bed. Ahem. To date she's an award-winning, acclaimed author of fourteen novels in romance and erotic romance, and happily calls writing her full-time job.

Kimberly has a bachelor's degree in social work and a master's in human relations and has held licenses in social work and mental health therapy in various cities within the United States and abroad. She volunteers at various social-service agencies weekly and is a long-standing member of Zeta Phi Beta Sorority, Inc., a community-conscious organization. Kimberly is a naturalist and practices aromatherapy. She believes in embracing the powerful woman within each of us and meditates on a regular basis. Kimberly would love to hear from you. Visit her at www.kimberlykayeterry.com.

Kimberly Kaye Terry

Hot to TOUCH

KIMANI™
ROMANCE

To my beautiful daughter who always inspires me to be the best that I can be.

 KIMANI PRESS™

ISBN-13: 978-0-373-86189-7

Recycling programs for this product may not exist in your area.

HOT TO TOUCH

Copyright © 2010 by Kimberly Kaye Terry

www.kimanipress.com

Printed in U.S.A.

Dear Reader,

I'm very excited to introduce you to Shane Westwood and Emma Rawlings. Writing their story was an absolute blast! Shane is a smoke jumper used to fighting extreme fires in the West, and Emma is a photojournalist who is always after the most dangerous stories. Yes, they are two hotheads! Two stubborn people who fight against love, but when they finally give in, boy, do the fireworks start! They took me from scaling walls, to jumping out of airplanes…to hot, sultry nights making love under a starlit sky. I hope you enjoy reading their story as much as I enjoyed writing it.

I loved the West so much that I decided to stay there for a while. Look for *To Tempt a Wilde*, book one in my new Wilde family series, featuring sexy alpha cowboys in Wyoming, coming out this spring. I appreciate your support and will do my best to continue writing hot, sexy, exciting stories featuring alpha men and the women they love!

Keep it sexy,

Kimberly Kaye Terry ;)

ACKNOWLEDGMENTS

To "Buck," Bruce Nelson:

The courage that you and your fellow jumpers display, the sacrifices you all make, is truly humbling. Your willingness to share your knowledge, point me in the right direction, and answer my emails at one o'clock in the morning and not choke me was truly amazing ;). Thank you, thank you, thank you!

Prologue

The roar of wind competed against the loud purr of the turbine engine, breaking the silence that otherwise prevailed inside the Twin Otter plane.

Butterflies fluttered in Shane Westwood's stomach as he sat hunched on the narrow bench, shoulder-to-shoulder alongside six other men, as the plane circled the dark column of smoke that rose from the blazing fire below.

He fingered the Celtic cross around his neck unconsciously, before tucking it inside his beige, Kevlar-coated jumpsuit.

The closer they flew to the billowing smoke, the more anxious he became.

His anxiety had nothing to do with the jump ahead, or the potential danger he and the others faced. Like a junkie jonesing for his next fix, Shane lived for the exhilaration and potential danger each mission would bring. After his first jump six years ago, he had logged in more than 125 jumps; 75 for training and 50 live fires.

No, his anxiety had *everything* to do with the fear that he wouldn't make it in time to save his best friend.

"Give us the go-ahead already, damn it," he spat out tersely into the microphone line in his ear, connecting him to the ground crew.

"The pilot doesn't have a clear landing shot, Shane… hold your damn horses, man, we'll get down there!" one of the support crew shot back in response to Shane's impatient demand. The drama of what was unfolding below was evident in his voice. Jumpers and ground crew alike were feeling the stress.

"*Get* us a clear shot…time is running out."

"We have to be at three thousand feet before it's safe to jump."

"Aww no…I think I'm gonna hurl!"

When he heard the man next to him moan, a rookie smoke jumper, Shane didn't bother giving him a second glance—not in the mood to give the rookie a pep talk.

The fact that the rookie was his jump partner for the mission hadn't sat well with Shane, but they were running low on jumpers as all the other available men were already on the ground.

He knew it was the young man's first "live" fire jump, and he knew that like most of them, rookie or seasoned pro, he'd either hang on or get the hell out. There *was* no in between.

No matter how much instruction you had, no amount of training could prepare a man for his first jump into live fire. It was as exciting as it was frightening. And, it was their way of life. Most men figured out pretty quickly if they had what it took to be a smoke jumper.

"Get ready, men, we've found a landing spot."

Shane swiftly stood, motioning for the others to follow. The spotter had identified an opening.

The plane flew with doors opened and Shane peered down, viewing over three hundred acres of red flames crowning the large spruce trees below, as the plane circled around the billowing columns of smoke, trying to find a safe spot for the men to jump.

His heartbeat kicked up a notch, his gut clenching at the sight.

The acrid, sweet scent of wood smoke filled the plane as air rushed in through the open door. Shane and the others quickly donned their masks and flipped down the heavy wire-mesh screens.

An unexpected bump of turbulence hit. Shane swallowed down the nausea that rolled through his stomach. Steadying himself, he grabbed the overhead cable.

The plane lined up for their initial pass over the identified target and the spotter threw the first set of drift streamers out to gauge the wind. The spotter turned to Shane and held up two fingers, giving the team the "go" sign. Everything looked good. Time to roll.

Shane acknowledged the sign, paused and glanced at his temporary partner. When the man nodded, letting Shane know he was ready, he turned back to face the door. As the senior jumper, Shane would be the first man out.

Despite the gear, Shane felt the heat hit his face as he stood at the edge of the jump door, his gaze sweeping the scene below.

When he felt the spotter's slap on his shoulder, he propelled himself forward, immediately starting a mental countdown "jump-thousand, look-thousand, reach-thousand, wait-thousand, pull-thousand…" he thought, his fingers curling around the rip cord as he jumped from the plane.

Timing it just right, he pulled on the cord, threw back his head and watched his bright orange-and-white-striped parachute balloon open with a smooth-sounding pop.

Shane yanked the toggles and faced into the wind for landing.

Steering his chute away from one of the flaming trees, he felt every muscle straining, sweat pouring down his face behind the mask as he fought against the pull of the wind, his chute violently swaying back and forth.

In less than a minute he'd be on the ground. And once he was, he'd have to hit it running. His concentration was fully on making a safe landing, but soon all other thoughts would have to be shoved to the side.

His best friend's life depended on it.

Chapter 1

Push off. Legs spread. Release. Push off. Legs spread. Release…

Shane leaned against the wall with his arms folded across his chest and studied the woman, his brow creased in concentration.

He ignored the activity going on around him and throughout the gym, his attention focused solely on the small figure several feet away, making her way down the faux-stone-covered wall.

One small, black-gloved hand was wrapped securely around the rope just above her at chest level; the other was loosely wrapped around the part of the rope near her backside as she made her way down the wall.

And what a backside it was.

Shane found himself staring at her curvaceous little

body in fascination as she rappelled the wall. His gaze shifted away from her round, firm buttocks—that even the shapeless khaki shorts she wore didn't disguise—to trail down her bare, dark brown legs.

Shane shook his head, berating himself for noticing her legs, sexy or not.

Although it had been too damn long since he'd been with a woman, this one was *definitely* off-limits.

This was the woman who'd managed to wrap his base manager around her finger and somehow convince him to allow her to do an "in-depth" story on him and his fellow smoke jumpers.

He tore his gaze away from the petite woman and glanced around at the crowded gym.

Although it was P.T., the time of morning when his men, if not on mission, performed physical training, apparently the base manager wasn't the *only* one taken with the reporter, Shane noticed, his scowl deepening. Several of his men were hanging around the rappelling wall, watching the reporter, nudging each other and pointing at her like schoolboys checking out a cute girl.

He pointedly stared and made eye contact with several of them, but his scowl didn't seem to scare them off. If anything, it seemed to encourage them. One of his men gave him a thumbs-up, jerking his head toward the woman, grinning his fool head off, as if Shane had something to do with her being there. Not even close, Shane thought, his irritation growing. And if he had his way she'd be packing up as soon as her curvy little body hit the ground.

He'd recently returned from a mission where he'd volunteered to help the short-staffed Alaska unit with a kicker that had blazed for twelve days before they'd gotten the fire under control. Afterward, he'd stayed on and helped with the massive cleanup.

Pleased with how it had gone, but beyond exhausted, a month later he was just looking forward to a little R and R. Preferably in the form of staying in bed for forty-eight hours with one of the always-ready, always-willing, long-legged blondes from the local town of Landers.

When Roebuck, his base manager, had first informed him on his way back home that he was allowing a reporter to come into the jumpers' camp to research an in-depth article on their lives, one that would possibly hit the national papers, Shane had been less than enthusiastic.

After the series of fires taking place over the last eighteen months across the coast, their small, sleepy community had been a hive of activity, gaining national exposure and bringing in a lot of media attention.

In particular there was the fire that had occurred near the start of the spree that resulted in two jumpers dying and the only female jumper on staff leaving. There'd been plenty of speculation as to why she'd left, but no one besides Roebuck, Shane and a few of the senior jumpers knew the real reason.

When Roebuck had explained his reasoning for allowing the reporter access, eager for a chance to show what he and the men did on a daily basis, a reluctant part of Shane had understood. The attention the article would bring, would give good press to their small base, and with it, much-needed donations to keep the satellite office up and running.

That was until he'd found out that Gene Raw was in fact Emogene Rawlings; that the reporter used the shortened version of her name on her byline.

His eyes narrowed as he watched her—"Emma" in person—carefully, but swiftly make her way down the wall, pushing away the spark of admiration he felt for her ability.

From his vantage point, he had an optimal view of her. He found his attention riveted on her small nuances—the way her brow furrowed as she scaled the wall, the way the full bottom rim of her lip was pulled between her top teeth, the small bead of sweat that rolled down past her temple, over her cheekbone and down the curve her of her cheek.

She quickly maneuvered her way down the rest of the wall. Once she made it to the floor, she spun around jubilantly and gave several of the nearby men high-fives.

"She's amazing, huh, Shane? I've never seen a first-timer go down the wall so fast!"

Shane turned to one of the jumpers who'd come to stand next to him. He nodded his head curtly and glanced around. He'd unconsciously moved closer as he watched her and was now standing a few short feet away from the rappelling wall.

"Yeah, she's a regular marvel." As soon as he made the snide remark, Shane wished he could retract it. The younger jumper frowned, a puzzled look on his face.

"Do you know her, Shane?"

Shane shook his head and turned to watch the reporter with narrowed eyes.

"I guess you gotta wonder about a woman like that," the man went on, oblivious to Shane's irritation.

"What do you mean?" Shane asked.

The jumper shrugged his broad shoulders. "I don't know. She's so small, looks kinda fragile to me. Wouldn't think a woman like that would be in her line of work. I guess I figured when they told us a reporter was gonna be following us around, living at the camp, I didn't figure it'd be a woman. Damn sure not one as fine as Ms. Rawlings."

When Shane raised a brow, the younger man blushed. "Well, you know what I mean," he murmured.

When the woman in question turned toward them, as though she knew they were talking about her, she and Shane locked glances. From his short distance away he saw her large brown eyes widen as he deliberately allowed his gaze to leisurely slide over her, from the top of her head down to her small, boot-covered feet.

When his eyes met hers again, he noticed the subtle once-over she gave him as well before her eyes darted away. But not before he saw the flush of red on her deep brown skin.

Chapter 2

He was the sexiest jumper she'd ever seen.

Although, truth be told, Emma had only been at the hub station for a short time and had never actually met a smoke jumper in person before her arrival. But, no doubt about it, this one was at the top of the food chain.

The jumpers gave new meaning to the term "alpha male," from the base manager all the way down to the new recruits. It was a prerequisite for the men in their line of work to be in top physical and mental condition, always ready to go into action when the call came.

For all that, there was still something *more* about this one; something indefinable. A hint of danger and a sharper edge surrounded him, clung to him, made him that much more…prime.

He was the kind of man who, if placed in a room with ten other men looking for a fight, would be able to take each of them down, one by one.

Emma shivered.

The minute he'd walked into the packed gym the back of her neck had prickled in awareness and she'd turned around in search of the cause. As she stood braced at the top of the rappelling wall, preparing to go down, she'd paused and watched him as he casually spoke to the others. When he had turned to face her, as though aware of her regard, she'd quickly looked away before he'd caught her gawking at him. Giving the jumper who was assisting her an absent smile, Emma focused her attention on the task at hand.

The jumpers, at first cool toward her, had slowly warmed up and had begun to take her seriously. She didn't want to erase the progress she had begun to establish by being caught eyeballing one of the men as if she were a starving woman and he a big, juicy steak.

She had been expecting that she would have to work harder to gain the respect of some of the men, coming in as an outsider and the only female in their close-knit brotherhood. She knew it would take more than the few days she'd been there, yet she'd been both surprised and pleased with the welcome they'd given her, so far.

Today was the first day they'd invited her to join them for physical training. She'd brought along her backpack that held her camera and mini-recorder, but she hadn't pulled either out.

A natural athlete, she'd been thrilled when one of the

squad leaders invited her to give the rappelling wall a try, a training they used to prepare themselves for their live missions.

Emma had scaled down some of the most intimidating mountains in the Himalayas while following a mountaineering guide from Nepal while writing a story on the Sherpas. So when one of the smoke jumpers invited her to try rappelling, she'd been more than confident in her skills.

She eyed the jumper who scaled the wall alongside her. Concentrating on the climb, she put thoughts of the newcomer from her mind and made short work of the twenty foot wall. She made it to the linoleum floor, spun around and grinned widely when she finished minutes before the other climber did.

Several of the men surrounded her, clapping her good-naturedly on the back. Her smile faltered when she again felt that odd prickling awareness slide along her skin. Glancing over her shoulder, her gaze collided with *his*—the jumper who'd entered the gym before she'd begun her descent.

He now stood just a few feet away, staring at her with an intensity that was unnerving. His light blue eyes were fixed on her, a deep frown on his face, pulling his thick, dark eyebrows together until they formed a straight line as he continued to stare at her...assessing her.

When she'd seen him enter the gym, she could tell he was tall, but now as he stood next to one of the other jumpers she could see that he towered over the other men. Dressed in a variation on what looked to be the standard uniform the others wore for physical training, on him it looked completely different. It was more earthy…more masculine.

He wore the standard-issue gray T-shirt that hugged his broad chest and wide shoulders and a pair of loose-fitting matching gray gym shorts that cupped his lean hips.

His dark hair was cut short, almost military short, save for the slightly longer length on top. Although he currently wore a deep scowl on his face, his wide mouth was sensual and inviting. He casually wore an aura of command that set him apart from the others.

Like a lightbulb going on, it suddenly dawned on Emma who he was. Shane Westwood. He was the second in charge, after the base manager, the one she'd heard so much about from the others. According to the men, he was the golden boy, the man who could fight fires single-handedly…a regular superman.

She'd also learned from one of the rookies that he was staunchly against any female smoke jumpers gaining membership into the small substation. When she asked why, the man had shrugged his shoulders, claiming not to know the answer.

But she knew there had to be a story behind it despite claims to the contrary. Her instincts practically screamed at her, telling her so. And Emma never ignored her instincts. But she let it drop, choosing not to alienate her new informant by digging for more information he wasn't ready to give.

When her eyes met his again, the look in them made her draw back physically. His animosity seemed to reach out and grab her, so vibrant it was almost as if it were a living thing. The effect was as though someone had punched her right in the stomach.

Emma forced her body to stay erect, forced herself not to take a step back, so sudden and unexpected was both the look and the effect it had on her. For whatever reason, he didn't want her there. Okay. Fine. She could deal with that.

What she didn't want to examine, much less deal with, was her body's reaction to him. The way—despite the obvious dislike he had for her, whatever the reason was behind it—the sizzle of awareness between them made her tremble slightly. She'd never had that happen with anyone else, much less someone who seemed to have such an irrational sense of disdain for her.

Whatever his issue, Emma had no intention of allowing him to try and get rid of her. She had come for one purpose, and one only—to write the best damn article she could, one she hoped would go to national syndication and take her career to the next level.

He was the senior smoke jumper at the station, and after the base manager, he was the one in charge. He had a lot of pull. His influence, if he chose to protest her presence, would make her job difficult.

Too much was on the line to allow some guy with a serious attitude—no matter how fine he was—to mess it up for her. She casually looked over her shoulder. A shiver ran over her arms as their glances collided again.

That might not be such an easy task.

She held his gaze until he broke contact, only to

allow his eyes to slowly, insolently run the length of her body. When his glance brushed over her breasts, she felt her body respond against her will. Her treacherous nipples stabbed against her sports bra, and Emma checked herself before she wrapped her arms around chest as though she had something to be ashamed of.

She wasn't wearing anything provocative. Before her climb she'd tucked her oversize T-shirt into her knee-length shorts and pulled her hair up into a ponytail, and she was wearing no makeup. Yet the way he was looking at her, she felt naked. Exposed. She suppressed a shiver.

She placed a purposefully nonchalant smile on her face before turning away, but she could still feel his eyes on her. If he had something to say to her, he could come and say it, she thought, ignoring the sizzle of heat searing a hole straight through her back.

"Have you had a chance to go over and meet Ms. Rawlings yet?"

Shane turned as the base manager approached, dragging his attention away from the reporter.

"*Ms.* Rawlings?" he asked, raising a brow. His commander's dark face flushed in acknowledgment of the emphasis.

"Listen, Shane, if I told you she was a woman, you never would have agreed to it."

"Damn straight."

There was a short pause, both men eyeing each other, neither one giving an inch. Finally, Roebuck sighed.

"Give her a chance. I've known her editor for years.

We go way back. If he says she can do the job, she can. We need the good press that'll come from her being here and the potential donations from the public. I don't have to tell you how tough the economy is. And the state budget is tight. This could get us the cash flow we need for new equipment. So please, play nice."

Shane was ready to fire off a retort, just as the woman approached them. He clamped his mouth shut, folded his arms across his chest and waited until she stood in front of them. Giving Shane only a quick, cursory glance, her eyes darted away and she turned her attention to Roebuck.

Up close, her small, heart-shaped face was dominated by a pair of large, dark brown eyes, surrounded by long, full lashes. As she'd scaled down the rope, he'd noted how long her shapely legs were, but he had misjudged her height. Up close, the top of her dark brown head barely reached him at chest level.

Both her height and pretty face gave the appearance of a fragile doll. Still, although petite, her legs were long, shapely, and toned, as was the rest of her body, belying the notion that there was *anything* fragile about Emogene Rawlings.

Several strands of hair had escaped from her haphazard ponytail, and Shane felt a sudden and unwanted need to finger the dark tendrils and see if her hair were as soft as it looked.

"That was damn impressive!" Roebuck said to her, pulling Shane out of his observations.

"Thanks, sir. I can't believe how much fun it was!"

"It's hardly fun and games," Shane said. "This is training—training the men go through on a daily basis to prepare them for whatever hazardous mission they may face on any given day. Call it what you will, but it's hardly fun and games."

Roebuck turned to Shane, heartily smacking him on the back. "Of course it isn't, Shane. And I think Ms. Rawlings will fit right in, no problem at all!" If the commander's hearty enthusiasm sounded a bit forced, no one called him on it. "And for the next four weeks, Emma will follow you, learn what it takes to be a jumper, interview the men and—"

"Now wait a minute, boss. What do you mean she'll be following *me?* I never agreed to that!"

There was a long, strained silence. "Shane, Emma… why don't we go to my office and discuss the particulars?" Roebuck turned on his heels, walking stiffly toward the exit.

Emma glanced around self-consciously, noticing they were the center of attention. With a tight smile aimed at the staring group of jumpers, she went to follow Roebuck out of the gym. From her peripheral vision she saw Shane hesitate, as though he had no intention of meekly following along.

She released a breath of relief when she saw him reluctantly follow them. So this was the jumper she was supposed to shadow. A sinking feeling settled in her gut.

Well, damn.

Chapter 3

"Sir, no disrespect intended, but I don't really give a damn what 'good press' she'll bring to the station. I just want her out of here. The sooner the better. And she sure as hell is not trailing me around. I have enough to worry about without playing babysitter to some damn reporter!"

Shane tried to keep his anger at a slow boil. He respected his base manager and didn't want to go off half-cocked and say something he'd regret later.

Although Roebuck was in his early forties, his craggy features made him look older, deep lines scoring the sides of his full mouth, due to the hard life he'd led. He'd come to the smoke jumpers after serving several years in the military as a paratrooper, most of his service done during several deployments overseas.

Despite all of that, Shane had rarely seen Roebuck blow his stack. Even when one of the younger jumpers screwed up, the captain always kept his cool and always treated everyone fairly, equally, from the newest jumper to the seasoned vets.

It was one of the many traits Shane admired about his commander, and one of the many reasons he willingly followed the man's lead, trusting his judgment, something crucial in their line of work.

But not this time.

He turned away, walking over to face the large bay window, not really seeing the view of the mountains and the hill country below.

"Shane."

When he felt a heavy hand on his shoulder, he turned his head.

"Be reasonable. It's a done deal. Nothing you can do about it. I've already given her permission." Roebuck sighed. "Look, I know where this is coming from. But you can't let one incident make you like this. It was an accident, no one—"

"She's not 'shadowing' me. Period," Shane interrupted, not wanting to hear what his commander would say next, fighting against memories of a time he tried his hardest to ignore.

"And I would think you of all people would understand why," he finished, grimly.

Emma paused, her fist poised to knock on the door, when the voices inside grew louder.

After leaving the gym on their way to the office, her cell phone rang, a call from her editor.

Although she could have allowed it to go to voice mail, she used the call as an excuse to get away. She needed a chance to pull herself together and rally her defenses against what she knew was a battle she faced with Shane.

Although she'd taken the call, she'd spoken less than five minutes with Bill before ending the conversation with a promise to call him back.

The anger of the prudent never shows.

She'd learned the value of the wise old adage long ago, while on her first assignment in a small village in Burma. She'd incorporated the saying as much as she could into her everyday life, although at times it wasn't so easy to do.

She took a deep breath, slowly exhaling. No matter what happened, she wasn't going to allow him to bait her into saying something she would regret later. He wouldn't make her say something stupid and shoot herself in the foot before she even got it in the door.

When she could no longer clearly hear the angry staccato of words, she strained her ears to pick up on the conversation, stepping closer to the door.

After several minutes of silence, Emma mentally and physically squared her shoulders and knocked briskly on the door.

So, tall, blond and fine didn't want her around his precious jumpers? Oh well. She had every right to be there. She hadn't been given any special favors, she'd worked hard to get the assignment and no one was going to take this golden opportunity away from her.

There was a slight pause before she heard Roebuck's deep baritone calling out for her to enter. Cautiously, she opened the door, plastering a bright smile on her face.

Like a magnet, her eyes were drawn to the jumper as he stood near a large window, his long legs braced far apart, big arms crossed over his chest, his back to her.

Roebuck motioned her to come inside. "Come on in, Emma. We were just discussing your assignment."

Emma picked up on the false cheer in his voice and the worried glance in the commander's eyes as he looked at her.

Obviously he was aware that she'd heard at least part of the discussion. Despite that, along with the accompanying tension so thick in the room she could cut it with a knife, Emma nodded and stepped inside the office, closing the door behind her.

The office was small, but everything was neat and orderly. An oversize, scratched, oak desk took up most of the room, upon which two monitors sat. One was a computer, and the other seemed like some type of weather-monitoring system.

"Have a seat, Emma. We can go over the particulars of the article. Your expectations and ours."

"What did you have to do to get this job?" Before Emma could take the offered seat, Shane spoke, surprising her, turning to face her.

"So you can speak. I thought you were just here for

my viewing pleasure." Before she knew it, her mouth started in, before her head could rule it out, the retort tripping off her tongue.

Shane's expression darkened, his brows nearly meeting in the middle as he took two steps toward her and stopped. "What is that supposed to mean?"

"Whatever you want it to mean." Emma shrugged. "Probably the same thing you meant when—"

"Shane," Roebuck broke in. "Emma, before this goes any further, let's all sit down, discuss this like we have some sense."

Emma fully faced Shane, her anger rising. She crossed her arms over her chest, keeping her expression light. "Well, you were asking me how I got the job?" she baited Shane. "Just what did you mean by that?"

"You call yourself Gene Raw, right?"

"Yes. And your point would be?"

"My point is you seem to be…billing yourself as one thing when you're selling something else entirely."

"I'm not *selling* myself as anything other than what I am. A damn good photojournalist." Emma brushed off his not so subtle innuendo and focused on the latter part of his sentence.

"I don't get how having a pen name makes me seem as though I'm billing myself—or as you like to say, 'selling' myself—in any way different than who I am." Emma stopped and drew in a deep breath. "And I do that purely because of men like you. Men who think that just because I'm a woman, I'm not as capable in doing my job as any other journalist. I don't have to—"

"Look," he interrupted. "I don't pretend to know how

it works in your world. I don't give a damn one way or another. What I do know is that lives are on the line here. There is no time for play, this is real—"

"And how will my presence here alter that?" Emma bit out angrily, her chest heaving, brushing against the hard wall of his abdomen.

She took a step back.

It was then that she noticed how close they stood to each other. One or both of them had moved so that they were so close they were touching. Emma caught the subtle hint of his cologne, mixed with his natural scent, wafting across her nose.

After backing up, she continued. "I didn't get any special favors to get this job. I worked hard for it, just like I have for everything I've ever gotten. Every accomplishment I've ever had was because *I worked hard for it*." She emphasized each word, unwanted emotion burning the back of her throat.

"No one gave me any special consideration." She made one more attempt at civility, desperately trying to bring her anger and threatening tears under control.

"I'm sure you did nothing to get any favors, *Ms. Raw*," he said, emphasizing her pen name. He just wouldn't let it go.

"Like I said, I got this job fair and square, Mr. Westwood. And unless you want a sexual-harassment claim slapped on you and the rest of this camp, I suggest you put on your big-boy panties and deal with it."

The back of her teeth hurt so badly from clenching them that she knew that as soon as she reached her room she'd have to pull out her industrial-sized, extra-strength Motrin to rid herself of the pain.

Turning on her heels, she strode toward the door. If the door slammed back against the hinges with more force than necessary, she didn't really give a damn.

To hell with not allowing her anger to show. If only he wasn't so fine.

Chapter 4

Shane threw his workout gear on the floor, and then grabbed his duffel bag from the chair in the corner and tossed it onto his bed. He yanked open the zipper and began to unpack, separating his clothes, his thoughts on the woman foisted on him by the general manager.

He still hadn't unpacked since his return. Although he had a place in town, he'd decided to stay at the station to keep an eye on the reporter.

He'd been so tired after coming home that the only thing he'd wanted to do was lie down for a week straight and not think about the fire that claimed the lives of three civilians or the havoc it had wreaked on the small Alaskan community. He certainly didn't want to think about the helplessness he'd felt watching families lose their homes, all their possessions, with nothing left but the clothes on their backs.

He didn't want to think of any of it.

No, he'd wanted to chill and put all thoughts of the fire and the destruction out of his mind, decompress after the physically and mentally draining ordeal and indulge in a little mindless rest and relaxation.

Well, that was shot to hell, he thought, dumping the rest of his clothes in the hamper in disgust.

From the moment he laid eyes on Emogene Rawlings, his gut told him she was nothing but trouble wrapped up in a little package, big brown doe eyes staring at him. She might have fooled the others with her demure smile, dimples flashing, but he caught the speculating look in her eyes when she didn't think he was looking at her. Sizing him up, no doubt, figuring out which angle to take to win him over. Even as he had the thought, he remembered the hurt look she tried to hide when he'd all but accused her of her sleeping her way to get what she wanted.

He felt a momentary stab of remorse, remembering the sheen of tears she'd tried like hell to hide. But he hardened himself against the look, and the way he'd wanted to apologize for the unnecessary remark.

It wasn't going to work, not on him. He was on to her game. Their heated exchange echoed in his mind, reinforcing his belief that the kitty definitely had claws.

As he unpacked the remaining items from his duffel bag, the image of her legs as she rappelled flashed in his mind's eye, her strong, lean muscles flexing as she pushed off the wall.

She had the kind of legs a man dreamed about, the kind he could imagine wrapped around his waist as he drove into her perfect little body.

"Damn!" he mumbled, shaking his head as though to purge the image of her long legs, along with what he wanted to do with them, from his mind.

He angrily dumped the few clean items he had into one of his drawers.

Before he turned from the dresser, he glanced down at the small, 3 x 5 framed picture, the only picture he had in his room. A ghost of a smile lifted the corners of his mouth, replacing his frown. He looked at the image staring back at him, of the two men grinning ear to ear, faces covered in soot, as though they'd just conquered the world. He ran a finger over the edges of the frame before lifting the photo from the dresser.

It had been taken not long after completing his training. He and Kyle had just returned from fighting a forest fire in Idaho, a grueling job that had taken three weeks just to get the fire under control. His glance slid to the woman directly behind them, the smile slipping from his face.

Ciara Summers. The woman responsible for the death of his best friend.

The memories hit him hard, replaying in his mind, reel by reel, as though from some old movie.

Shane hit the ground, removed his chute and took off running. Ignoring the yells from the others to stay clear, he went after Kyle, who was trapped inside one of the remaining cabins in the decimated area.

Through the roar of the blazing fire, Shane made it to the cabin and heard his friend's frantic call for help to save Ciara. After pulling the woman outside to safety, he turned around to head back to the cabin, despite the commander and other jumpers yelling for him to stay clear, that the cabin was collapsing.

The memories played out in slow motion. He stood, frozen in place, watching in disbelief as Kyle lay trapped beneath a fallen column, flames shooting in every direction around him.

Surrounding him, the hungry flames were eating the cabin alive when it finally shattered in a fiery explosion, collapsing in on itself, debris flying everywhere.

And then there was silence.

Shane carefully placed the frame back on the dresser.

Emma was just like Ciara, and no woman was ever going to get close enough to interfere with his work again if he had anything to do with it. Nothing had ever been the same again for Shane; the guilt ate at him just like the hungry flames that devoured his friend.

"Deal with it, my ass," he said, gritting his teeth. "Round one is yours," he said, aloud. "But, I'll have you out of here before the week is out."

As he made his promise, he ignored the inner voice that mocked his proclamation.

Chapter 5

As soon as she walked inside her room, Emma allowed the backpack to ease from her shoulders. Barely making it to the corner chair mere feet away, she slumped down into it lazily.

She untied the laces of her Timberlands and, using the toes of each foot, pushed one and then the other boot from her aching feet, kicking the shoes away. With a groan she lifted a foot into her lap. She sighed, massaging her instep before bringing the other foot into her lap and repeating the deep massage.

What was it about her that always made her attack any new thing she was told she couldn't do?

After leaving Roebuck's office too angry to think straight, she'd wandered into the gym. She'd felt as though every man's eye was on her, feeling as though the words between her and Shane had spread like proverbial wildfire throughout the station. The word was out.

Shane Westwood didn't want her there.

The men who'd begun to open up to her now turned away as she entered the gym. When one of the squad leaders approached her and asked if she wanted to participate in training with a few of them, she agreed, ignoring the way a few of the rookies nearby snickered at the comment.

Once outside, she scanned the course. At first glance it didn't appear *impossible* for her to maneuver; she'd run courses before. This one reminded her of an obstacle she'd once done at a military post while doing a story on fighter pilots. Large, it spanned at least a quarter of a mile in length. Much like the military obstacle course, it was filled with rope ladders, high walls to scale and logs to run across, and at the end of the course was a rope swing where they'd have to jump over a pool of water to reach the other side.

Feeling confident to the point of cocky, Emma strutted over to where the others were gathering. A pin was stuck directly into her balloon of confidence when one of the squad leaders placed a large duffel bag at her feet, telling her to suit up.

"Suit up?" She frowned, speaking to his retreating back.

"You have two minutes to put on your jumpsuit and protective gear, including helmet, and then place the duffel bag on your back." As he spoke, Emma swiftly began to don the suit, her eyes widening as she spied the heavy gear inside the bag.

"After the whistle blows, you have ten minutes to maneuver the course. This is the first of many trials for this particular test before your examination, rookies. Don't screw up."

Emma was seconds away from backing out, eyeing the heavy helmet in her hand and the even heavier duffel at her feet, when she felt a prickling on the back of her neck. She didn't have to turn around to know where the source of the now familiar sensation came from.

Mentally squaring her shoulders, she completed suiting up in the allotted time. When the whistle blew she was off and running with the others.

"Carrying a friggin' twenty-five-pound rucksack, wearing another ten pounds of gear while tripping over tires and going facedown in a pool of water in an obstacle course...*what* in the world was I thinking?" Emma wondered aloud, reflecting on her afternoon.

But she knew what made her accept the challenge. It was for the same reason she went after any new challenge, particularly one she was told she couldn't do. She didn't need any psychotherapist to give her an unneeded, expensive, in-depth analysis.

It wasn't that she'd been abused physically as a kid. Instead she'd been ignored, or tolerated at best. Left on her own, she'd never had many friends, being shuffled from relative to relative. She learned to rely on herself and herself only, determined not to need anyone to take care of her.

That transient way of living, picking up and moving frequently, had also made it so that she'd never needed a "home." If she occasionally thought of what it would be like to stay in one place longer than a few months, of having somewhere to call home, she reminded herself that she had the type of life she'd always wanted—an exciting career, traveling, experiencing the world on her own terms.

After completing the obstacle course, her body dripping with a combination of sweat and water from the headlong dive, she nearly collapsed as soon as she made it to the other side. Despite it all, she'd found herself grinning her face off, proud that she'd beaten several of the other rookies who'd started with her. A movement to her left caught her attention and she spotted Shane on the sideline with a few other men, his focus solely on her. Their gazes locked.

Emma inhaled a swift breath. The way her pulse quickened, heart banging against her chest, had nothing to do with the physical act she just completed and everything to do with the man who was watching her.

Emma caught the glint of admiration in his bright blue eyes before he turned away.

Groaning, Emma settled back against the headboard, crossed her legs and dragged her bag from the floor before plunking it down beside her.

She took out her cell phone, flipped it open and saw that she'd missed two calls. Without looking she knew that both had to be from her editor. She didn't really have anyone else who would call her. Particularly because of her lifestyle, she had next to no one she actually called "friend." The few she did were reporters or photographers and led a similarly transient life, and rarely made idle phone calls just to chit-chat.

And that was the way she liked it, she reminded herself.

When she'd spoken to her editor earlier, their conversation had been brief; she hadn't gone on to detail her experience with Shane. She'd assured him everything had been going "peachy," and then there'd been a pause and Emma had held her breath. Bill was one of the few people who could pick up on how she was feeling, no matter how hard she tried to hide it from him. Although he hadn't called her out, just gruffly said, "good," she knew she wasn't off the hook.

"Might as well get this over with," she mumbled.

She quickly punched in his number, the only one she knew by heart, and waited for him to pick up the phone.

After several rings, a gruff voice on the other end barked, "Hello."

"Hey, Bill, it's me." Emma leaned back against the headboard, sighing deeply.

"You sound like hell."

"Way to make a girl feel good," she replied, laughing humorlessly.

"Been one of those days, huh?"

"Yeah, you could say that."

"Humph. I was wondering when you'd call. How's it going so far? You all settled in?" Emma heard the concern he tried to hide in his scratchy voice. Asking if she was settled in was his way of asking what she needed from him. Not *if* she needed anything, but *what* she needed. Emma knew that whatever it was she needed, he'd do everything in his power to help her. He never actually came out and told her that he worried about her, that he cared, it wasn't his style, but Emma knew he did.

Bill Hanley knew her better than anyone, including her own family. He'd been the one to give her her first job, right out of journalism school. He'd also been the one to give her her first overseas assignment.

He was the first person to believe in her abilities as a reporter—even during the times she doubted them herself. Emma was determined not to let him or herself down.

"Yeah, Chief, I'm cool. I'll let you know if I need anything."

There was a moment of silence. Emma was about to disconnect the phone when he surprised her. "Look, if things get funky, let me know. You don't have to put up with bull. I know some folks," he said, and she smiled.

His phrasing reminded her of an old mafia flick. Bill had an old-school way of speaking, straight and to the point.

"Is there something you neglected to tell me?" She shut her eyes, allowing her head to rest back against the wrought-iron headboard.

There was a slightly short pause before he spoke.

It was small, but enough that it made her fatigue melt away and alertness take its place.

"Bill?"

"The base manager and I go back, way back. I once did a story about his firefighter unit in the army, back when he was in the military. We became friends and have kept in contact ever since."

"And?" she asked when he paused again.

"And…about two years ago he lent his help to jump a fire in Alaska. There was a lot of talk surrounding the fires that he and several of his men helped to fight. Rumblings about negligence on the part of senior personnel, to jumpers ignoring direct orders from the general manager. One jumper died and one was pretty badly injured. As far as I can remember there was a lot of talk about a female jumper in particular. Someone blamed her for one of Roebuck's jumpers' death."

"What was the name of the jumper who survived? The male jumper?" she asked, although she already knew the answer before Bill opened his mouth.

"Westend…Westwood. Shane Westwood, if I recall correctly. Why?"

Emma was silent. The feeling in her gut worsened. "And the woman, who was she?"

"Can't remember her name offhand. After the dust settled, last I knew she was transferred to another station."

Emma's instincts screamed at her that Shane was the cause for the female jumper leaving.

"Don't tell me…this is the guy who you're shadowing?'

"Yeah. And he wants nothing to do with women," she said. "Well, at least not on his turf. And if he has his way, I'm on the next flight out of Lander." Emma blew out a tired breath. "Maybe this assignment wasn't the best one for me."

She felt an overwhelming sense of defeat, a desire to just say, "Whatever" and let it go. She was so tired of fighting. Tired of having to prove herself over and over.

"Since when did you let the way others feel affect you going after a story?" Bill asked gruffly, after a long bout of silence. "Look, you're one of the best photojournalists in the business."

"It's not that. I know I'm good," she said and laughed. "I don't mean it like that."

"Well, you should," he replied firmly.

"You know what I mean."

"I do, and you are. Not a damn thing wrong with being sure of your abilities. You've been on back-to-back assignments for the last six months. Maybe you need to relax, take some time off—"

"No, I can handle it," she interrupted. "I just need to unwind, take a long bath and hit the sack…get my mojo back," she tried to lighten the mood, laughing lightly. She knew she hadn't fooled her editor one bit—the man knew her too well—but thankfully he let it go.

When she disconnected the phone she pushed away from the headboard, a thoughtful look settling over her face, contemplating the information Bill had given her. Another piece to the ever-growing puzzle that was Shane Westwood.

Chapter 6

Emma was awake before her alarm could go off, feeling refreshed and ready to take on whatever challenges Shane Westwood could dish out.

The jumpers' days started early. Immediately after breakfast, everyone gathered in the ready room where the day's agenda was set in a general meeting with the hub's crew. Although the job of conducting the morning meetings was the senior jumper's, Roebuck had conducted them over the last two days as Shane had been away.

Emma donned the black sweats that had become her uniform and then sat down on the bed to pull on socks and her Nikes. Neat by habit, she quickly made the bed and walked across the room to the small refrigerator in the corner.

Not normally a breakfast person, Emma was happy to find that the room came equipped with a refrigerator, which she'd stocked her first day at the station with all of her favorites from a nearby convenience store: milk, juice, assorted muffins, diet soda and Captain Crunch. She didn't know what the day held in store, so she decided to forgo the bowl of cereal and diet soda in favor of a small carton of juice and one of the bran muffins instead.

Twenty minutes later, she was opening the door to the ready room, the raucous sound of the men inside reaching her ears before she stepped in.

Her gaze swept the room until they connected with the one man who she hadn't been able to get out of her mind over the last forty-eight hours.

"Let's go. Roll call!" Shane called out in a booming voice, his voice drowning out the din of chatter as he faced the waiting, assembled men. The room quieted within seconds.

"For those of you who didn't know, I'm back. It's good to see you all again. The commander briefed me on what happened during my absence. I heard a lot of great things—I'm proud of the job B crew did in assisting the Montana jumpers during a cleanup job... great job, guys!" he began.

"For those of you joining us after hiatus, welcome back. Hope you had a restful time off while the rest of us worked our asses off," he said, and they all guffawed good-naturedly, slapping several of the ones who'd had time off on the back.

He then turned to a small group of rookies who

stood to his left in formation. "And I haven't had the thrill of meeting you all yet. Don't worry, that will soon be rectified. We'll be getting to know each other very well over the next six weeks," he said, and several of the older jumpers openly scoffed.

"Now, let's hit the agenda. There's a new mandatory class on preventing fires, which is basic, I know." He held up a hand when several groaned. "But it's mandatory, so no complaining about it. Also, there's a weapons-certification class for those who plan to or want to continue to carry guns. Remember, nothing smaller than a .357 magnum. Don't beat your chest and go caveman on me, it's not a field trip. It's mandatory games policy. C crew, that means you guys. Last time I checked, most of you were due for recertification. Don't shoot the bears unless they're coming to eat you," he yelled out to the men who began to file out.

One of the squad leaders jumped onto the raised platform, joining him, and yelled out, "All rookies— outside. NOW! Don't know why y'all are here any damn way! Roll call is for smoke jumpers, not freakin' wannabes!" His booming voice echoed throughout the room, as loud and intimidating as any army drill sergeant's. The rookies wasted no time. Within minutes they fled from of the room.

Shane was in the process of speaking with one of the squad leaders when a prickling sensation crept across the back of his neck, coiled around his body and pooled in his gut.

Emma Rawlings had entered the ready room.

Shane turned, his gaze sweeping over the heads of the room and the fleeing bodies of the rookies before connecting with hers.

With only a slight pause, he continued the briefing. When asked a question, he reluctantly broke contact and answered. When he turned back around, one of the jumpers had come to stand beside her.

His eyes narrowed when he saw her withdraw a pad from the oversize bag she wore, busy scribbling notes. She placed the notebook back inside and then withdrew an expensive-looking camera, brought the lens to her eye and snapped off a shot of the jumper she was speaking to before aiming her lens toward the men gathered around her.

When a few of the guys turned toward her, and actually smiled for the camera, Shane knew he had to turn away or he was liable to go over and snatch it from her hand to further prevent his men from embarrassing themselves with their shameless display of eagerness.

"Each group has their general assignments for the day. Before heading out, check the board for further assignments. Any more announcements?" he asked, turning to the squad leaders. When none answered, he continued. "Roll call!" and proceeded to fire off the list of names to answering variations of "Yo," "Yep," and "Huah!" until everyone had been accounted for.

When several stopped on the way out the door to stand and talk to Emma, he barked, "I'll meet with C team in the cargo area in ten. Ms. Rawlings, I need to speak with you."

* * *

When the last man left, Emma had no choice but to face him, watching him approach warily while reminding herself that anything he could dish out, she could take.

When he stood less than two feet away from her he crossed his arms over his big chest. The stance, like the scowl on his face whenever he was around her, was becoming irritatingly familiar.

"Looks like you've met all the men."

The way he said it made it seem as though she had stripped down and given each man a lap dance instead of the simple interview she'd conducted. She gave him a tight-lipped smile, refusing to let him see how badly he was getting to her.

"When the men are being briefed, I'd appreciate if you wouldn't distract them," he continued and stepped closer.

Emma took an involuntary step away. Her glance slid over his sensual mouth, one side hitched lightly in a mimicry of a smile as he stood there, looming over her.

She stood still. Like a doe caught in headlights, she felt hemmed in. The air around them grew thick, moist—dewy with an underlying tension she couldn't break away from. She refused to back up even when he stepped so close she could smell the heated, musky scent of his aftershave mixed with his natural male essence.

She blew out a breath, slowly, her lips partially opening, her tongue snaking out to lick the lower rim. When his gaze followed the action of her tongue, Emma's heartbeat began to thump frantically against her chest, her palms grew moist, her body hot.

Emma raised her chin, resisting the urgent desire to flee. "They seem like big boys. They can handle it, I'm sure."

He raised a hand and brought one finger down the line of her jaw. She stared up at him, controlling the crazy desire to turn into his caress.

"Didn't your mama ever tell you that playing with fire is a sure fire way to get burned, Ms. Rawlings?"

With their gazes locked, his bright-eyed gaze roamed over her face, over her mouth and down her throat before meeting hers. Emma felt as though it were his hands running over her, her body responding against her understanding or will.

The ends of his nostrils flared, his mouth following the path of her tongue as it again wet her lips.

"I'm working with the men this morning. I'm afraid you'll have to find someone else to entertain you, Ms. Rawlings."

When he walked away, she expelled the breath she hadn't been aware she'd been holding.

God, what in the world had just happened, she wondered, her body slumping back against the wall.

Unconsciously running her fingers over the part of her face he'd touched, she watched him stride from the room.

Chapter 7

"I'm training the rookies this morning. Meet me in the classroom in fifteen minutes."

Emma spun around upon hearing Shane's voice behind her, trying not to allow her surprise to show. She assumed that after their exchange two days ago she'd be left to her own devices, and this idea had proven correct over the last couple of days. She hadn't been idle during that period, had instead used the time to interview and photograph the jumpers as they trained, pleasantly surprised when the majority seemed eager to speak in their down time.

She'd only caught occasional glimpses of Shane, usually by accident. And nine times out of ten, Shane was out the door within minutes whenever she showed up. Maybe Roebuck had spoken with him, or maybe he'd had a sudden change of heart regarding her. Whatever the reason, Emma wasn't going to look a gift horse in the mouth. With a nod, she quickly made her way to her room and grabbed her gear, just in case. She was back in the classroom before the allotted fifteen minutes was up.

When she showed up to find she was the only one there, none of the rookies around, she felt a keen sense of disappointment. The disappointment led to outrage when one of the squad leaders strode into the room and informed her that she'd be watching a series of films about the history and lives of smoke jumpers, followed by a training film on the various ways a parachute could kill a person.

"You have *got* to be kidding me," she murmured, her mouth thinning into a long, angry line as he set up the film.

"Oh, and uh, Shane said to leave you with this." He handed her a small, hot bag full of popcorn.

When he caught the look in her eyes, he quickly turned and left, but not before Emma saw the smirk lurking in the squad leader's eyes. Tempted to throw the bag of popcorn at his retreating back, she instead plopped down in a nearby chair.

"The least he could have done was leave me some extra butter to go with it," she mumbled moodily.

"Fighting fires of any type is a tough, dirty job. Only the brave need apply…"

As the narrator of the black-and-white film spoke, she sighed, settling back in the chair and reaching into the bag of popcorn.

* * *

In the ready room, after the marathon of dusty old archived films she'd been forced to sit through, Emma finally had enough and left, seeking out one of the squad leaders…and avoiding Shane.

She hadn't known what in the world the man would throw at her next. Still, for every roadblock he threw in her path, Emma had maneuvered around it, pleased with the progress she'd begun to make on her article.

Initially she'd been relieved for the reprieve, but as the days grew, her irritation grew as well. She needed his input as second in command. She was supposed to be trailing him, after all. She didn't need his approval, and his insights were what she needed to make her article shine.

And although she'd managed to do her job without his interference over the last two days, she decided then that it was time to flip the script.

After her afternoon interview with Roebuck, again left to her own devices, she'd gone into the gym, only to see Shane along with his team, working out. She turned to beat a hasty retreat when he caught sight of her and *invited* her to go against one of the senior jumpers in scaling down the wall.

"Ms. Rawlings." He stopped her before she could take more than a few steps.

Reluctantly, Emma turned back around to face him.

"You seem to know your way around a wall," he began, and several of the men chuckled. Emma lifted her chin, raised a brow and waited for him to continue.

"Rick here is one of the best. Care to match your… skills…against his?"

The man he nodded his head toward was built like a truck. Although equal to Shane in height, this man looked as though he belonged on a football field battering through an angry defensive line, instead of jumping out of planes.

"You beat him, you have free rein of the station." He threw out the challenge. "Nothing is off limits."

"No *one* as well?" She saw the hesitation in his eyes and waited.

Finally, he nodded. "Nothing." He paused. "And no one. But if you lose, you lose your article as well."

The stakes were high, but without Shane Emma realized she didn't have a complete article anyway. She dropped her pad and took her place at the top of the wall and then glanced over at her competitor and bit her lower lip.

There was no way she could she beat this man, she thought, inwardly groaning, but she put on a confident smile nonetheless.

She grabbed the rope, and seconds before Shane blew the whistle she slid a glance his way. She hid her surprise when he gave her a very deliberate wink and side grin before quickly turning away.

Her smile grew. Maybe she could do this after all.

After she beat the giant smoke jumper, her feet touching the floor moments before his, she spun around, searching for Shane. She ignored the sting of disappointment when there was no sight of him, and she gave a half smile to one of the squad leaders who congratulated her on her win.

She then wandered outside, camera in hand and ready to catch the smoke jumpers in action as they trained, again impressed with the unit's training ground.

Separated by open grassy areas stood a two-story army-type barracks where most of the men stayed, housing the jumpers, jumper pilots, as well as the recruits. Although most of them didn't live at the station full-time, the base had facilities to house the one hundred personnel who lived and worked there.

The men were busy doing a variety of jobs—from sitting in a storage area wrapping water containers for freight to engaging in physical readiness training.

Yet no matter how mundane the job, Emma could feel the hint of expectancy in the air, as though they were ready, on alert. It was their prime season, the time when anywhere, at any time, a fire could rage and they'd be on the next plane headed out.

When lunchtime rolled around, Emma decided to forgo the commissary where most of the men ate and instead head to her room.

"You don't seem like the type to be afraid of much. Kinda remind me of myself when I was your age. So, what's the problem?"

Surprised to hear a deep yet feminine voice coming from directly behind her, Emma spun around. A woman sat there, casually eating a muffin, behind the glassed-in partition area that separated the office from the waiting room.

A frown settled over Emma's face as she stared through the glass at the older woman.

"Excuse me?" she asked, taking a hesitant step forward.

When the woman lifted a nearby mug of coffee to her mouth and took a healthy swallow, eyeing Emma over the large mug without speaking, Emma moved closer.

"Uh…do I know you?" she asked, watching as the woman lifted the muffin to her mouth again, took a hefty bite, nearly biting it in half and chewed thoughtfully, her eyes narrowed at Emma.

The older woman delicately dusted the crumbs from the tips of her fingers.

"Name's Isabelle. Friends call me Belle. I work the desk from time to time. Get's me out of the house," was Belle's way of introduction, holding out her hand.

Emma racked her brain trying to remember if she'd met the woman and had forgotten. In the time since she'd met Shane her thoughts had been so occupied with trying to figure him out that it was possible she had obliterated memories of meeting the woman completely from her mind.

"I was the one you spoke with before you came to the station… I'm a friend of your editor."

"Ohhhh, *yes,* Ms. Belle!" Emma smiled, walking forward to shake her hand, finally remembering. "Wonderful to finally meet you in person!"

Isabelle Stanford had been helpful when Emma and

Bill were coordinating the best time for Emma's stay, and the two of them had several telephone conversations with the older woman. Belle had been a part of the Lander station from the moment it was built. Her husband was one of the first jumpers at the station and later served as the general manager.

When he passed away several years ago, Roebuck, who'd served as a senior jumper under his command, had asked her to come and help out at the station. Emma had heard the fondness in her voice when she shared the information with her.

The two women spoke for a while before Emma asked, "Ms. Belle…what did you mean about 'my problem'?"

Isabelle shrugged her wide shoulders and adjusted her glasses, perched at the end of her nose, peering at Emma so long she grew uncomfortable beneath her penetrating gaze.

"Lead me, follow me, or get out of my way. That was one of my husband's—God rest his soul—favorite sayings. It was a saying of General Patton."

Emma frowned. "I don't get the point."

Isabelle gave Emma a look that made her cheeks flush in embarrassment. She didn't know the older woman beyond the phone conversations they'd shared, yet the look she gave her wasn't hard to read. Emma felt inexplicably foolish.

"Well, seems to me that you came here for a story. A damn good one, too. But that's not gonna happen if you pussyfoot around, acting afraid of your own shadow. The young woman I spoke with on the phone didn't give me the impression that was the way she… How do the young folks put it?" She stopped, her brows coming together in a line of concentration. She snapped her fingers. "Roll! That's it! Didn't seem like that was how you rolled."

Emma didn't know whether to laugh or be embarrassed at the woman's assessment. But she understood what she meant, and she couldn't argue with it. That wasn't how she rolled, and she was going to have to do something to change it. After a few more minutes of chatting, Emma left with a promise to catch up with Belle later.

After lunch, Emma sought out Jake, the jumper training the rookies that day, and followed him out to the training ground, still thinking of the older woman's words.

She swiftly jotted down notes, trying to capture the flavor and essence of the intensity of the training, soon lost in the writing and excitement of the story that was unfolding on her notepad.

Feeling as though she was being watched, Emma turned to see that Shane, along with one of the squad leaders, was addressing a group of rookies who were not training. As the other man spoke to the young jumpers, Shane's attention was on Emma the entire time.

The intensity of his gaze was so sharp that it was as though his fingers were skimming over her face, down the line of her throat, instead of his eyes.

Her nipples hardened, stabbing against her bra when his gaze brushed across her breasts. Her breath caught on a soundless gasp, and her heart thudded against her chest. He finally broke eye contact when the squad leader spoke to him.

Emma released a breath she'd been unconsciously holding in a silent *whoosh* of air. Closing her eyes briefly, she opened them and gave a fleeting look around, in dread, knowing that every man on the field had to have just witnessed their silent exchange. She sent up a silent prayer of thanks when she realized they were all busy with their individual training, no one giving her or Shane any attention.

"Getting some more good stuff for your article, Emma?"

Startled, she spun around, grasping the railing in support when Roebuck spoke beside her. She had not heard his approach, her entire awareness only focused on Shane.

"Sorry. I didn't mean to startle you," he apologized and grasped her elbow to help steady her.

"No, no, it wasn't you. I was just watching the men. I must have gotten so caught up in writing I was lost in my own zone," she replied with a shaky laugh.

His eyes darted to the ground near her. Bending down, he casually picked up her pen, lying near her feet where she dropped it during her "deer caught in the headlights" moment with Shane. Emma felt her cheeks flame as she accepted the pen with a meager "Thanks."

She cleared her throat, wondering how long he'd been standing there watching her without her knowing.

"You mentioned you used to do some long-distance running?" he asked.

"Yes, back in high school I ran long distance. Got a scholarship for college as well."

"Good. I thought you might be interested in coming over to watch a potential new class while they run. That and a few other physical tests are part of the elimination process to see if they qualify for the next rookie class. Interested?"

She hesitated. She was growing tired of simply watching from the sidelines, something she seemed to be doing a lot of lately.

"With forty-pound sacks in hand. Thought maybe you'd be interested in participating with the others," he said.

"With a forty-pound sack?" She grinned.

"For a mile. Timed. Wanna give it a go?"

From her peripheral vision she saw Shane, not far away, watching them. Noting the scowl cross his handsome face, she grinned up at Roebuck. "Try and stop me!"

Emma was laying faceup on the ground, staring at the sky, wondering what possessed her to take Roebuck up on his challenge. Again that irritating little voice inside her head reminded her why: Shane Westwood.

She waved a limp hand in front of her face as though to swat away the nagging voice, before weakly resting her hands back down on the soft grass. After a moment, she pushed herself back into a sitting position, preparing to stand, when a large shadow stood directly in front of her. She brought a hand to her face to shield her eyes, peering up.

She barely prevented her eyes from rolling as she stared up at Shane, waiting to hear what he had to say about her less-than-stellar performance running with the sack. When his hand reached down, she hesitated briefly before placing hers in his and allowing him to pull her to her feet.

"Go ahead and say it," she said, dusting her hands down the sides of her legs, not looking up at him. "I was terrible."

When she heard what sounded like a laugh from him, she looked up to see a small grin tugging at the corners of his lips.

"I wouldn't say terrible. Certainly not good, but not terrible."

Emma felt her own lips twitch in response to his unexpected humor.

"Whichever it is, you did a hell of a lot better than a lot of others," he said, and she turned around to see that there were still several of the others just finishing the course as they spoke.

"And definitely a hell of a lot better than I did the first time I tried," he said and laughed again.

"You? No way!" she said incredulously, dusting her hands down the front of her shorts some more.

"Yeah way. Came in dead last, if I recall. In fact, my partner had to come and get me for the last quarter mile and drag my sorry butt the rest of the way. I got beat by two girls and an old man. I was lucky they gave me another chance and kept me on. I was pitiful."

Emma didn't know whether to take him seriously or not, until she saw the gleam of honesty in his eyes. His self-deprecating humor surprised her. It was at odds with the confident, no-nonsense exterior he presented to the world. Or one he presented to her, at any rate.

Maybe the lighthearted side she glimpsed was the real Shane, the one he rarely showed, yet hovered beneath the surface, ready to break free.

"Truce?" He struck out his hand for her to shake.

"I wasn't aware we'd been fighting." She tilted her head to the side, as though considering his offer. "So, truce it is," she agreed, placing her hand within his. The minute they touched, a small arc of electricity flared between their joined palms, as if with that handshake they'd suddenly reached a turning point in their relationship.

His smile wasn't quite a full smile, just a slight lifting of one side of his sensual mouth. But her heartbeat leaped in her chest at the way it transformed his face, the smile making her wonder if a truce were a good idea or not.

Chapter 8

"Yes...mmm..." she moaned in a husky whisper.

Her soft, throaty sounds of delight filled the room.

Shane glanced down at her through a hazy vision of lust and sweat as she moaned, her head tossing back and forth on the pillow while his hand cupped and molded her firm, taut breasts.

He lightly pinched one of her nipples, watching in lustful fascination as the chocolate-brown nub pearled. Unable to resist, he leaned down and replaced his fingers with his tongue, capturing it between his teeth, wondering if it tasted as sweet as it looked.

"Hmmm. Delicious." He mouthed the words against her.

He bit down gently and she cried out sharply, her

body bowing, arching into his caresses. He swirled his tongue, savoring her unique flavor.

With his legs tangled around hers, he felt her sweet cream trickle along his legs.

"Are you ready for me?"

He held his breath, waiting for her to tell him she wanted him, wanted him as badly as he wanted her.

She captured his face between her hands, forcing him to look at her. "Are you ready for *me,* Shane?" she asked, turning the tables on him.

Instead of answering, he grasped his phallus and ran the tip between her sweet, wet folds.

Her swift breath told him she knew his answer.

Spreading her legs, he shifted her until their bodies were in perfect alignment and slowly, savoring every moment, began to slide into her warm, welcoming body…

A loud shrill forced Shane's eyes to snap open, his heart hammering in his chest, his own hand wrapped around his erection as he was yanked out of his dream.

With a curse, he glanced down at the empty space beside him on the pillow, the dream still achingly vivid his mind.

Although it had been a dream, he could still see her, smell her…taste her.

With another curse, he shoved away the tangled sheets that were bunched around his waist. He slammed a hand over the beeping alarm before heading to the bathroom to take the coldest shower of his adult life.

* * *

In her own bed, Emma woke with a cry tumbling from her lips as her alarm went off, forcing her out of her dream, very similar to the one Shane had just had.

With a sigh of defeat, she reached over the side of the bed, picked up her running shoe and threw it at the alarm. She watched in satisfaction as it tumbled off the table and silenced, landing with a thud onto the floor.

"I can't get away from him, not even when I sleep," she muttered.

Emma stared sightlessly up at the ceiling, trying to block out the memories of the dream and how good Shane had made her feel; how alive she'd felt from his touch.

If Shane could make her feel that good in a dream she didn't know that she could handle what he'd do to her in real life. With a curse, she lifted the pillow from beneath her to cover her head, as though to smother out the hot images that lingered in her mind.

Chapter 9

He hadn't had sex in six weeks, four days and—Shane glanced down at his watch—roughly four hours.

A Nickelback song blasting from speakers scattered throughout the bar and greeted Shane the moment he stepped inside.

He glanced around, surveying the scene. He'd come here for one reason and one reason only: to find a willing woman for the night and forget everything, and everyone, including Emma Rawlings…if only for a few short hours.

Although discriminate in his choice of sex partners, Shane wasn't the type to go without for too long. The first thing he normally did after a mission was seek out a willing woman within twenty-four hours of settling in, particularly after an adrenaline-pumping mission like the one he'd recently returned from.

The fact that it had been over a month and he hadn't, *had* to be the reason that Emma had appeared nightly, like clockwork, in some of the dirtiest, *wake-up-with-his-shaft-in-his-hand-wishing-it-was-her-who-held-him* dreams he'd ever had.

After their declared truce and subsequent time spent together over the course of the last week, she'd invaded his head during the day and his dreams at night, destroying any chance he'd had of keeping an emotional distance from the beautiful journalist. That is, if he ever had a chance in the first place, he thought, walking toward the bar area.

There was also the attraction that, even though he'd tried to ignore it—as if ignoring it would make it go away—was so palpable, so damn hot and tangible, Shane didn't know how much longer he could stand being around her without acting on his impulse to take her to the nearest bed and make love to her until neither one of them knew their own names. Maybe that would get her out of his mind, out of his dreams. One time would be all he would need to exorcise from his thoughts the growing desire he had for her.

He ordered a drink and leaned back against the bar, looking over the crowded dance floor filled with gyrating bodies. When the bartender set his beer in front of him, he lifted it to his lips, allowing the bittersweet liquid to pour down his throat, his thoughts still on Emma.

There ought to be a law against the way she filled

out a pair of running shorts. Or the clench in his gut he got every time her dark brown eyes lit up, coupled with the shy smile that curled the ends of her full lips when she accomplished a task.

He had it bad and he hadn't even seen it coming. The attraction he had for her had snuck up on him, and damn if he knew what to do with it.

He set his beer down on the bar with a thump.

The hell of it was, he knew the attraction wasn't one-sided. He picked up on her body language whenever she was around him. He'd caught the sidelong glances she'd cast his way when she thought he wasn't looking; the way her eyes would darken, the unconscious way she would moisten her lips when he stared just a bit too long at them. Unwillingly fascinated...the attraction was there, palpable. And mutual.

She wanted him as badly as he wanted her. Double damn.

The way she stood up to him fed the growing admiration and attraction he felt for her. There was something more in her gaze, besides her attraction to him and her all-around stubbornness. Something she hid well from the others. Something she had obviously practiced hiding, he thought. In the depths of her brown eyes was an uncertainty she tried hard to cover up. Yes, she showed herself as a more than competent woman, had a confidence that most lacked, yet lurking beneath the confidence was an odd vulnerability.

When he'd been pushing her the last week, he'd been pushing at that vulnerability he had picked up on. Hoping to use it against her, hoping it would make her break. Make her go away and leave him and his men alone.

To leave *him* alone.

With the firm support she had from Roebuck, along with the grudging respect he noted she'd been steadily gaining from the men, he knew getting rid of her was out of the question. And, if he were honest with himself, he was no longer sure he wanted her gone.

Not yet, anyway. Not until…

He'd only messed up in judgment once with a woman, and it had cost him dearly. His jaw clenched as he forced the memories away. Shane tipped back the bottle of beer, lingering thoughts of Emma refusing to go away.

In his mind, snapshot images of the way the sweat made her T-shirt cling to her body, molding her high, firm breasts to perfection, sprang into thought.

He shook his head, trying to clear away thoughts of her. He wasn't going there. He didn't want to think of her or the way he felt whenever she was within ten feet of him…or anything else that would interfere with the reason he'd come to the bar. Not tonight.

No, tonight he would put both the mission he'd returned from, along with the troublesome woman, firmly from his thoughts. He glanced around, broodingly surveying the scene. It was an eclectic place, a place where a desperate housewife needing to get away partied with a Brooks Brother–wearing executive, looking for a little action any way they could get it.

The large dance floor was packed with gyrating bodies getting their dance on, to an old Michael Jackson

tune, with an abandon that was testimony to it being a
Friday night and there being plenty of alcohol pumping
in their systems.

Multicolored lights flickered off the walls from the
large strobe suspended from the ceiling in the middle
of the dance floor. Split-level, the first floor played a
mixture of music and had a large dance floor with bar
areas scattered throughout. The first level was what he
and most others referred to as the "meat market," the
place to hook up.

The second floor featured another dance floor—this
one smaller, along with a several games tables and the
prerequisite bar areas as well.

For those who wanted a more intimate place to hang
out, the new owners had created a third level on the
roof, with music, drinks and an even smaller dance
floor; a place where couples usually went to talk and
drink.

For his purposes, the main level was what Shane
wanted.

The partygoers all mingled; social status meant
nothing here. Those out for a drink and open to whatever came their way mingled with everyone else, all
looking for a hole to fill, a temporary solace to whatever
they'd faced the previous week.

Shane knew the feeling.

Within moments of his entry he'd caught the eye of
a few good prospects. As he drained his beer, he did a
quick assessment. His gaze collided with a big-breasted,
stiletto-shoe-wearing blonde who sat with three equally
beautiful friends.

He tilted his head, bringing the beer to his lips as she gave him a slow "come and get it" smile. Instead of walking over to her, he nodded his head in her direction. The wattage on her smile dimmed the smallest bit, but Shane didn't really care.

After spending a week chasing around one woman, he had no intention of continuing that method of interaction with another. After another minute, he saw her shrug, drain her glass and saunter his way.

"I don't think I've seen you around here. Come here often?"

Shane surveyed the leggy blonde with the husky voice, his glance falling to the pack of cigarettes in her hand. Unlike Emma, whose slightly husky sexy voice was due to genetics, the blonde's was attributed to years of smoking, no doubt, his glance casually noting the fine, shadowy lines around her heavily made-up eyes and long slashes scoring her thin lips.

He wouldn't normally go home with a smoker, but tonight he didn't care.

He eyed the rest of her in a casual once-over. A set of never-ending legs housed a pair of shorts so skimpy that part of her round behind was exposed. Her midriff-baring halter exposed a belly with a small diamond that shone brightly, the gem catching the lights from the club. The upper swell of her large breasts was so high, he could put a table runner over them and set his drink on it. The way she was eyeing him, her thin, red-painted lips parted wide and practically screamed that she was his for the taking...just the type of woman he was looking for, for the night. Someone uncomplicated and who wouldn't challenge him at every turn. The exact opposite of Emma, who continued to plague him, to invade his thoughts even when she wasn't around.

He took a healthy drink from his bottle and set it on the bar beside him. "Not often." He gave the blonde his full attention. "Can I get you something?"

Her laugh was strangely high compared to her voice, and a bit grating. Shane winced.

"Yeah, but, what I'd like from you isn't on the menu, sugar." Her bold gaze traveled over his as she stepped closer, her hand resting on his arm.

Just what he thought. No beating around the bush with this one.

"I'll have to take a rain check. I'm meeting some of my boys tonight."

Shane wasn't sure who was more surprised by his response, him or the blond woman, particularly as he had come to the club with the intent of indulging in the activity the blonde's eyes promised he'd get.

With a shrug and a "your loss" look, the woman wasted no more time with him. She turned, catching sight of another prospect two bar stools down and walked his way, putting enough sway in her walk to put a seasoned pro to shame.

Shane turned back to his beer, lifting the bottle, but didn't drink.

What the hell just happened? He'd come for only one reason: to find a woman and get laid. When the opportunity arose, he acted like a scared schoolboy out on prom night and backed out.

In disgust, he drained his beer and rose from his

stool. In his current frame of mind, he wasn't going to get what he came here for. He might as well cut his losses and head back to base.

On his way to the exit he glanced over at the dance floor and stopped in his tracks.

Laughing, talking with one of the young rookies, was Emma Rawlings.

His loins came to blazing life as the nightly dreams he'd been having, the kind that would put any teenage boy's wet dream to shame, came racing back into his mind.

Turning, he made his way slowly back to the bar, rethinking his decision to leave. When the bartender came over to ask if he wanted another drink, he shook his head no, pointedly. He needed a clear head.

Positioning himself in a prime spot, he kept his gaze on Emma.

When one of the rookies had invited Emma to go out, her first inclination had been to turn him down, wanting nothing more than a relaxing bath after what she thought of as a week straight out of hell.

Shane had made it his mission to make sure she'd give up. From the physical training to the hours spent watching dusty documentaries on anything from fire hazards to how to strap on a protective gas mask… not to mention the harrowing time in the mock smoke chamber, where she felt like she'd coughed up a lung— the man was relentless in his effort to push her. To prove she couldn't handle it.

But with every push she gave back everything she

had. Their battle of will created such tension that by the end of the week she no longer knew who she was trying to prove herself to—him or herself.

Despite the truce Shane had declared, Emma was more than a little disappointed with herself at the way she had taken to thinking of him nonstop, even when he wasn't around.

She shoved the tantalizing images of the two of them locked in an erotic embrace from her mind. She was tired and didn't really feel up to doing any self-psychoanalysis.

"Looks can be deceiving. What this bar lacks on the outside, it more than makes up for inside," a voice promised, cheerfully, bringing her out of her thoughts.

She glanced up at the rookie, Jake, who was smiling down at her.

Wanting to foster good feelings between them, needing the men to feel comfortable enough around her to talk to her, to open up about their lives so she could write an in-depth, hard-hitting article, Emma had agreed to go out with Jake and the others, even though she'd only wanted to fall into bed.

She eyed the large, warehouse-looking bar skeptically when they first approached it.

"Well, we're here…no use turning around now," was her less than enthusiastic response to the bar's appearance.

"You'll love it. I promise it," Jake said as he'd cupped her elbow and guided her toward the entrance to the bar.

"There's the rest of the crew. Let's go." He motioned to the small group that waited near the door.

She greeted the other rookies, along with the women that accompanied them. A popular song blasted from within. Once inside, Emma was surprised at how spacious it was. From the outside she'd been expecting… well, she wasn't quite sure what she'd been expecting. But it definitely wasn't what she saw.

"What do you think?" Jake asked over the loud music, guiding her farther inside along with the others.

"This looks great!" Although she spoke loudly, she doubted he could hear her over the pounding music vibrating off of the walls.

"One of the guys got here early and held a table for us."

Once they'd settled in and everyone had been introduced, she smiled when Jake pulled out her seat for her.

Emma carefully shifted her body away when he sat down next to her, pulling his chair closer, his hand lingering on the back of hers. She didn't want the impression given to the others that she was Jake's date.

"I just ordered a round of beer. It should be here any minute," shouted the man who held their table, just as a waitress appeared and placed mugs on their table, along with a huge pitcher filled to the top with beer.

When Jake handed her a drink, she shook her head, wrinkling her nose.

"I don't really drink beer. Never acquired a taste for it," she said.

"What do you want, then? I'll get you whatever you drink. Sky's the limit," he said and gave her a wink.

"Just a Coke is fine."

"Aww, come on, Emma. Loosen up. Have a big-girl drink!" one of the women said, and she laughed.

"Okay, how about a rum and Coke, hold the ice?"

"Now that's what I'm talking about!" Jake replied.

Although she agreed to the one "big-girl" drink, Emma wasn't about to lose sight of her objective, although she *was* having fun. One drink wouldn't hurt, she thought.

After Jake's return, Emma nursed the drink, laughing and joking along with the others until, one by one, several of the group coupled up and left the table, seeking out the dance floor.

"So, what's your story?" Jake asked, speaking low, his warm breath fanning her ear.

Emma resisted the urge to move away and instead took a sip of the drink, giving herself time to answer.

"I'm not sure that I have a story," she answered honestly. "I'm just here on a job."

Someone brushed past her chair, pushing against it and jostling her. Jake reached out a hand to steady her. Again, Emma gently moved away. From the corner of her eye she caught the way he frowned at her action.

"It must be exciting doing what you do. Traveling all around the world, chasing after the next big story."

"It can be," she agreed, before taking a sip of her drink. Placing it down she said, "But, who am I telling that to? Your choice of career is definitely no walk in the park. Why did you choose to be a smoke jumper?"

He laughed, shaking his head at her. "No shop talk tonight. Let's just have fun!"

Emma wanted to keep it light, but her reason for going out with them had been twofold—to keep up the good feelings with them so that they'd open up to her *and* get them to talk to her.

When the music changed, the fast, upbeat tempo giving way to a slower song, many others got up, wrapped arms around their partners and made their way to the dance floor.

"Would you like to dance?" Jake asked, turning to Emma.

"Me, oh, no. Thank you, though."

At his crestfallen expression, Emma softened her rejection. "It's not you. It's just that this week has been hard. I just kind of want to chill, you know?"

She ran a glance over his face. The proverbial tall, dark and handsome, Jake was normally the type of man she went for. She told herself the reason he was hands-off was because of her job, ignoring the taunting voice in her mind that called her a bald-face liar, as she instinctively thought of Shane.

"Aww, come on, Emma—"

"I'll dance with you!" One of the last remaining single women at the table piped in, and Emma released a silent breath of relief.

"Well…" Jake hesitated, his dark eyes darting back and forth between the young local girl and Emma.

"No, please, don't mind me. Go ahead!" She encouraged him, trying to sound casual but desperately wanting him to go.

"You sure you don't mind?"

"Positive. Go on and dance!"

Left alone, Emma turned restless eyes to survey the dancing crowd. When the waitress came by with a fresh drink, she shook her head no. She'd barely finished the last one and wanted to pace herself.

She stretched, twisting her torso in her seat and grimaced when she felt a slight pang in her side. Her muscles throbbed from the physically intense week, and she decided to stand up and try to get the kinks out.

Leaving the table, she walked toward the dance floor and stopped at the rail surrounding it, watching the others as they danced.

God, she looked good enough to eat.

Shane's glance rolled over Emma as she leaned against the sleek metal railing separating the dance floor from the sitting area.

She wore a simple black dress, but there was nothing simple about the way it clung to her curves. Used to seeing her in either workout gym shorts or after-hours jeans and T-shirt, he wasn't prepared for what she looked like in anything else.

The bodice of the dress molded to her breasts and clung to her stomach, accenting a waist so small his fingers itched to see if his hands could span it around completely. The material clung to her rounded hips, the hem of the skirt flirting at the tops of her bare, shapely legs.

On her feet she wore strappy high-heeled sandals, whose ties wrapped up her feet and tied at her trim ankles.

He'd watched as one of the rookies, Jake, had sat next to her, his arm draped casually over the back of her chair. The satisfaction he'd felt when she subtly adjusted her body away, angling herself in the other direction, was one he was no longer interested in denying. It wasn't doing him a damn bit of good trying to deny what was between them, anyway.

When the members of her table had left her all alone, he'd decided to make his move. It was time the two of them resolved what was between them, what refused to go away, no matter how much either one of them ignored it.

"Women don't belong here. You don't belong here. It's nothing personal."

Emma turned away from the crowd and stared up at Shane. In the dark club lights, he was able to make out the slight tensing of her body as he spoke, could feel the guard she seemed to put out, despite the nonchalant look that crossed her face.

"Last time I checked, this was a public bar. And women are welcome. In fact—" she leaned close as though whispering a secret "—women are quite the commodity here."

"You know what I meant," he said, and came to stand near her at the railing.

"Yes, I do know what you meant. But, you know what, Shane?"

"No, why don't you tell me?"

"I'm getting tired of the whole hot/cold treatment. What is it with you and women anyway? What happened to the truce? Aren't we beyond this now?"

Before he could answer, she held up a hand. "You know what?" She shook her head and stopped. "It doesn't matter. I came here to have good time. And I've decided I'm done trying to prove myself to you, anyway. Arguing with you is not only futile, but ridiculous. I think I'd rather try and reason with an uptown broom with a bucket on its head than all of this back-and-forth with you anymore. I've had enough!"

After she spoke, they stared at each other. Moments later, Shane started to laugh, and soon Emma joined him.

Once their laughter had subsided, holding his side, Shane asked, "What in the *hell* does that mean anyway, and where did you hear it?" which caused her to start chuckling again.

She wiped the tears from her face caused by her laughter. "God…I don't *know!*" She sniffed, shrugging a shoulder, a smile lingering on her face. "It's just something one of my relatives I once lived with used to say. Don't know which one, there were so many of them."

The smile, the one that made his heart thud against his chest, flashed, softening her expression. She was still smiling when he placed a finger beneath her chin. Startled, she glanced up at him, questioningly.

"What?" she finally asked, when he said nothing, a curious look on his face.

"There were so many you can't remember?" he asked gently.

At her frown, he clarified. "So many relatives you lived with?" His chest tightened at the bittersweet smile that replaced the sweet natural one from moments before.

"There were a few," she replied nonchalantly. Shane cursed himself when he noticed the tension stiffening her body, her defenses rising.

He ran a hand over his head, spiking several strands over his head.

"Look, I didn't come over here to harass you."

"Could have fooled me," she said, and turned away to watch the dancers on the floor.

He placed a hand on her arm, turning her back around to face him.

"Can we talk?"

"It's too loud to talk here. And before you ask, I can't leave. The others would wonder where I went."

He breathed a sigh of relief at her answer. She didn't say she didn't *want* to talk to him, so maybe he could somehow redeem himself, climb his way out of the confusing mess he'd created with her.

"Come with me. We don't have to leave the club. I'll have you back before the others even notice you're gone."

"Like I said, I can't leave." Emma bit her bottom lip as though considering.

"There are two more floors. The second floor is a bit smaller, but the top floor is even more relaxed. Much more quiet. A good place to have a conversation."

When she still hesitated, he held out his hand. "Please."

She drew in a breath and placed her hand in his. Shane grinned. "I promise. You won't regret it."

Chapter 10

Emma doubted she wouldn't regret it, but she followed him anyway.

Shane linked his arm through hers as he navigated them through the enthusiastic crowd and down a long hallway. He stopped when they reached a small elevator at the back of the narrow corridor.

"This way," he said, pointing inside.

After going up two short flights, the doors of the antiquated elevator squeaked open and they stepped out.

Again, Emma was shocked—pleasantly so—as she looked around. Unlike the other two levels teeming with partygoers, this one was less populated, the music muted, with a more subdued, relaxed atmosphere, much more to Emma's liking.

"Wow, this is amazing."

In the middle of the enclosed roof was a sitting area, sprinkled with lounge chairs and small settees, all nestled around a cozy-looking, white-washed brick fireplace.

Couples milled around the open area. Most were arm-in-arm with a glass of wine in their free hand. As she followed Shane farther inside, she stopped suddenly, her eyes widening.

"That's...different." She stopped in front of an oversize chair, big enough for two.

Pearl-white, the opening was carved in an oval, the plush pillow seat a bright canary-yellow. The chair reminded her of an overgrown egg.

"This used to be an old warehouse. And before that, if the rumors are correct, it was a disco. The new owners took over a few months ago and totally renovated the old place, found a few retro-type pieces at an auction and kept some of the old stuff around, too."

"It's different," she said, looking around. "But it's cool. I like it."

She allowed him to walk her farther inside before they stopped at the bar.

"Can I get you something to drink?"

"No, I think I've had enough. But, thanks." She turned away, looking over the small dance floor, tapping her foot in time to the upbeat music.

He held out a hand for her to take, "Dance with me, then?"

She'd spent the greater part of the last few weeks trying not to think about what it would feel like to be in his arms. It had been hard enough over the last week, following him, the two of them constantly in each other's company. Did she really want all that good angst to go up in smoke by purposely jumping from the frying pan into the fire?

"Come on. I won't bite. Unless you want me to," he said, and Emma laughed along with him at the cheesy line.

She placed her hand in his and allowed him to draw her to the dance floor. The music had changed, blending smoothly into one of her favorite old-school songs, the tune haunting her as the singer crooned about love gone wrong.

He pulled her against his body and wrapped his arms loosely around her waist. After only a moment of hesitation she reached up and looped her arms around his neck, glad she'd chosen to wear the one pair of high heels she'd packed, as it made it easier to reach.

Their bodies fit together as though they were made for each other. Her hips aligned with his, her breasts molding to his lower chest. Emma glanced up at him. His eyes, bright, fathomless, stared down at her, his expression unreadable.

After a moment of hesitation she laid her head on his chest.

She felt a subtle change in his hold; his arms tightened around her body, and his fingers boldly moved down her back, landing in the curvature of her waist as he moved with her, swaying in time to the music.

For a long moment they simply danced, their steps naturally in sync as they gave in to the music. Emma allowed the moment to be what it was, *enjoying* it for what it was. A simple dance.

"You look beautiful tonight," Shane whispered in her ear.

"Thank you. It's been a while since I got dressed up, much less went dancing."

He maneuvered them around a particularly enthusiastic couple, bringing her body closer to his in the process. They danced easily together, moving in small circles. It felt good, right, dancing with him, his hard thighs pressed intimately against hers, his strong arms wrapped around her waist.

"When I first heard about the jumpers, I was a wannabe thug. Young. Stupid."

Emma drew in a surprised breath at the unexpected disclosure. She lifted her head from his chest and glanced up at him but said nothing, simply waited for him to continue.

"I grew up in foster care after my mom…died," he said with a slight hesitation. "I wasn't the best kid. I did a bunch of stupid crap." He laughed, low and humorless. "I got in trouble, cut school a lot and got caught up with the wrong crowd."

The music changed. The new song was still slow but was more upbeat in tempo, yet they remained close and continued to dance slowly, their bodies intimately shuffling from side-to-side.

"One night I went out with my friends. We took a couple of six-packs and we headed to a cabin we'd found on the outskirts of town. It was just supposed to be a bunch of us getting together, having some beer and goofing off."

Emma felt the tension in his body as his arms tightened around her.

"What I didn't know was that the guys had other plans. It seems the old man who owned the place had pissed off our self-proclaimed leader, Rob. The old man owned a liquor store in town and wouldn't sell him any beer. Rob decided it would serve the old man right if we burned his place down. I didn't know what they had planned. Had no idea the old cabin even belonged to anyone. I thought it was abandoned."

"What happened to it, Shane?" Emma asked hesitantly when his jaw tightened.

Although his voice and face remained expressionless, being so close to him, she saw the remorse in his light blue eyes, the muscle tic in the corner of his sensual mouth belying his neutral expression.

Emma wrapped her arms tighter around his neck.

"They ran off after they set the place on fire and left me there. I couldn't leave, couldn't let it happen. But there was nothing I could do but watch. I was stupid. I should have left with them. There was no way in hell could I stop the fire. It was already spreading too fast," he said, his voice gone rough from emotion.

"The old man's place wasn't too far out. I ran and ran until I found the nearest cabin and called the fire department. The smoke jumpers came as well. The fire had grown. It was spreading to the forest, and the fire department couldn't handle it alone."

Emma laid her head back on his chest. She felt her

own chest constrict from the pain she heard in his voice and saw in his eyes.

"I was scared out of my mind. One more misstep and I knew I was headed for juvenile hall. After I called it in, I ran away. I—"

"You were the only one there, they would've blamed you. If you stayed, you would have gone to jail…maybe prison," Emma broke in.

"Yeah, well, I felt responsible. All of his possessions… a lifetime of memories were gone. I ended up turning myself in anyway."

The song ended, blending into the next, and they continued to dance, oblivious to what was going on around them. "After it was over, I was sent to juvy, just like I thought." She felt his shrug. "It was what I deserved."

"And the others? What happened to them? Did they go to detention hall as well?"

"No. They never got caught. Besides, I was just as much to blame as they were."

"But they were just as guilty. More so."

"Yeah, but at that point it didn't matter to me. I deserved whatever I got," he replied grimly.

Although the other boys were the ones in the wrong, it was obvious to Emma that Shane held himself accountable. But in her mind he had been a young boy who got caught up with the wrong crowd and made a poor judgment call.

"One of the smoke jumpers came to my hearing. His name was Kyle. He was part of the crew that cleared the area. After the judge asked if I had anyone to speak up on my behalf, Kyle stood up and asked the judge for leniency. It was the first time anyone had done anything like that for me."

Although they continued to dance, their steps slowed down to an easy shuffle back and forth.

"What happened then?"

"I was given a reprieve. The judge ordered five hundred hours of community service. Kyle asked that the service be with him, that I work off my community service at the smoke-jumper station outside of Lander. It was the best thing that ever happened to me. He saved my life."

The faraway look in his eyes had cleared as he glanced down at her. Holding his gaze, she allowed him to lead her away from the floor, his arms tight around hers. After they finished dancing, with his arm still draped casually around her waist, they walked toward the lounge area, both lost in their own thoughts. Emma felt a new intimacy between them—Shane sharing a part of his story was him inviting her into his private world, one she sensed he didn't share with many.

When they passed one of the odd-looking "egg beds," she gave it an extended glance. Noticing her fascination, Shane stopped. He jerked his head toward the bed. "Wanna go inside? Looks comfortable, if a little odd," he asked, one side of his mouth hitched up in a half smile.

Emma was tempted, but after a few seconds of indecision she shook her head no. With the thoughts she'd had running through her head lately about Shane, she knew a bad idea when she saw it.

"Hmmm…I think I'll pass on that," she answered, laughing softly, her humor self-directed.

"Scared?"

She relaxed into the curve of his arm when she caught the very devious twinkle in his eyes.

"Who me? Not even!" she grinned widely up at him, relieved to see the haunting expression from moments before fade from his eyes. "A gal just knows trouble when it smacks her in the face."

"Is that how you see me, Emma? As trouble?" Although spoken lightly, Emma felt the stiffening of his arm around her waist.

He pulled her around so that they faced each other, his arms still around her waist.

Emma couldn't look away from him. His piercing gaze pulled at her, sucked her in as though he were trying to see right through her. She drew in a shuddering breath.

"No, I don't see you that way at all. I see you as a man who's been through a lot."

Not quite aware of her actions, Emma reached out and ran her hand softly down the line of his lean cheek, her gaze locked with his.

"One who will protect those he cares about. One who will protect those he doesn't even know, at any cost. The kind of man I admire."

Emma spoke so low Shane had to lean down to hear her over the music. Yet the impact from her words were as though she'd shouted them. Her expression was soft and her eyes held a gentle understanding, accepting him for who he was, flaws and all.

He closed his eyes against the sight.

Taking her hand from where it lay against the side of his face, he turned her palm toward his and kissed the center.

He brought a hand up to the nape of her neck, tunneled his fingers through the soft hair at the base of it and brought his mouth down to meet hers.

The minute his mouth lay claim to hers it was as though a fire let loose.

He heard her moan against his mouth as he tugged her closer, until their bodies were flush against each other, the heat of hers pressing intimately against him.

Every moment he'd watched her over the last weeks, every wicked dream he'd woken up to, pushed into his mind. The way he'd imagined she'd feel beneath him... None of his erotic dreams compared to the real thing.

Even with clothes on, he felt every lush curve against his body. Her hands, soft and hesitant at first, brushed across his face, making him stir in his jeans as she leaned into his kiss. There was no one but the two of them at that moment. The noise and people surrounding them faded away.

Her sensual, full lips pressed against his as he played with her mouth, licking his tongue over their fullness, lightly biting the slightly fuller lower rim.

"God, your mouth is addictive," he murmured against her mouth, breaking the kiss.

Tilting her head to get a better angle, he pressed his

tongue past her lips and fully invaded her mouth. Once inside, it was he who groaned this time. The soft, velvet length of her tongue greeted his, wrapping around it and tugging, artfully playing with him.

She wrapped her arms more securely around his neck, tugging his head down closer, inviting him completely in as they explored each other.

Equally greedy for the other's touch, their kiss went nuclear, becoming a sensual battle of stroking tongues and lips, their mutual hunger exploding in passion.

His underlying hunger rose sharply the longer they kissed. His hand at her waist moved, traveling around the luscious curvature of her waist and cupping her firm, round cheek and squeezed.

She moved her body against his, pressing her breasts into his chest. Shane felt the stab of her nipples against him, in direct parallel to the hardening of his erection aggressively pressing against her soft stomach.

He felt a slight push from behind as someone brushed against them.

It was then that Shane became aware of where they were.

Slowly the noise from the bar broke into the intimacy they'd created, and he released her, resting his forehead against hers briefly before pulling away.

He placed a hand beneath her chin, angling her to look up at him.

The lids of her large eyes were droopy and low, her full lips made even fuller from his kiss, stained red and lush, inviting…begging for him to take them again.

She raised her large eyes to meet his. The stamp of sweet sensuality on her face made his erection harden to painful proportions. "You want to get out of here?"

"Let's go."

Chapter 11

Emma came out of the light doze with a start, jumping out of the cooled water, her eyes snapping open.

The knock she'd heard grew louder, and she glanced around, searching for the radio clock she'd placed near the tub.

"God, I must have been tired," she groaned, noticing the time. It was after midnight and she'd been in the tub for nearly an hour.

Quickly draining the tub, she rose and grabbed the towel on the chair, scrunching up her nose as she glanced down at her prune-like, wrinkled fingers.

After coming back from the club with Shane, she'd had her world turned upside down and sideways, and she still didn't know what in the hell had happened.

She'd quickly found Jake and gave a rushed expla-

nation that she wasn't feeling well and needed to leave.
When he'd offered to take her home, she assured him
she could make it back to the station on her own,
encouraging him to enjoy the rest of the night and that
she'd already called a cab, which was now waiting for
her.

She'd met Shane at the door and followed him
outside to his truck. The drive back to the station had
been quiet, the conversation forced, at best. The air of
expectancy and the tension were so thick her gut had
twisted into a series of knots. Finally she'd given up
trying to come up with conversation, instead staring
out the window as he sped along the nearly deserted
streets.

When they'd reached the station he'd dropped her off
at her room, saying he would see her in the morning,
leaving Emma at her door, bewildered and more than
a little frustrated, wondering what had happened.

After the way he'd opened up to her…and, God,
the way the man had kissed her, she had been fully
prepared for…

She shook her head. She didn't understand him.
Period.

One thing she did know was that his on-again, off-
again treatment was getting real old, real fast. She
sighed, pushing the depressing thoughts away, and rose
from the bath.

She swiped an oversize towel from the hook and
brushed it over her body before donning the flimsy robe
near the hook, slipping her arms through the sleeves.

"I'm coming, I'm coming!" Not bothering to try

and locate her slippers, she hurried from the bathroom while cinching the ties to the robe tightly around her naked body.

She opened the door a fraction, peeking through. Standing on the other side of the door was Shane, his broad back facing her. For a minute she was tempted to slam the door shut. Her emotions—or her libido, for that matter—couldn't take another dose of Shane Westwood tonight.

"I, uh, just got out of the bathtub. And it's late…is this important?" she asked, ready to close the door.

At the sound of her voice he turned, facing her. His eyes went to her mouth. Emma felt the heat instantly flame in her cheeks. Against her will, she felt her nipples surge, beading against the thin fabric of her robe.

She knew he couldn't see her well through the small crack, yet she clutched the lapels of her robe, bringing the ends tight against her throat.

"I know. I won't take much of your time. Can I please come in, Emma?"

Wary, she paused, before nodding her head and opening the door for him to come inside.

When Shane walked in, his gaze swept around the small room before he finally turned and faced her.

"Look, I came here to apologize. I can't explain what happens to me whenever I'm around you. It's like I become an entirely different person. I—" He stopped, at a loss for what to say next.

He took a step closer to her and stopped when she stepped back.

"Can we start over?"

Earlier tonight, he'd disclosed things he never had with anyone else to her. She'd gotten got inside his head more than anyone, and he was still trying to figure out how.

He felt like a rookie on his first live fire mission whenever he was around her. Ready, but his gut tied in knots.

He moved closer, until he was less than a foot from her. This time she didn't retreat.

His gaze hungrily brushed over her body. Her smooth, rich chocolate-colored skin glistened with dew from her recent bath, the dark color beautiful against the flaming-red robe she wore.

The amber glow from the small lamp on her bedside table highlighted her, clearly outlining her perfect, nearly naked body. His body hardened to a nearly painful degree when he noticed her dark nipples jut beneath the robe, poking against the thin fabric.

His lust for her was getting out of control. He reached out and brushed the backs of his fingertips over one satin-covered breast, over the nipple that extended, growing harder beneath his fingers. As though in a trance, he leaned down and covered her breast with his mouth through the silky material.

She exhaled a long, sweet sound that blew over his senses like warm rain as he pulled her tight little nub into his mouth. Through the thin, silky fabric, he felt her nipple, hard against his tongue. He finally released it and had to steady her as she swayed on her feet.

"Shane…" His name came out low and husky. He dragged his gaze away from her perfect breasts and sought her eyes.

"God, you're beautiful."

Her lips parted and her tongue swept over the full bottom rim. Shane dragged her unresisting body close and felt the steady thump of her racing heartbeat against his chest. He leaned down, running the side of his face against her neck. Her scent, a unique feminine mixture of soap and flowers and woman, assaulted his nostrils, surrounding him.

He pulled away, brought his hand to her face, stroking the soft skin of her cheek, his fingers trailing down the line of her throat. He stopped at the lapels of her robe. He held her gaze, the two of them locked in a sensual web, the air around them growing thick, heady, palpable with lust and need.

One finger toyed back and forth across the soft, smooth skin at the crest of her breasts before he retraced his path—his hand snaking around her neck, his fingers tunneling into her hair—and lowered his head. A whispery breath of need escaped her partially opened lips seconds before their lips touched.

With a low groan, Shane pulled her tight, molding her sweet curves to his. His hands moved down her body, past her waist and over her rounded hips before skimming the silk-covered surface of her behind.

Impatiently, he placed his hands beneath her robe, pushing it to the side and exposing her, his hand moving past the skimpy material of her panties and cupping one round, firm cheek.

He swirled his tongue around her welcoming mouth before hollowing it and lapping it against hers. A sharp, aching hunger for her rose, sharp and immediate. He stroked the satiny skin of her bottom as he explored the slick heat of her willing mouth. She released a whimpering cry that echoed within his mouth.

His erection strained against his jeans, growing thicker, harder, the longer they kissed. When he felt her nipples tighten and spike beneath the skimpy robe, felt her frantic tugging on the back of his head to draw him nearer, he pulled away.

He rested his forehead against hers, both of their breathing labored.

"No...wha...what?" Emma cried, wrapping her arms tighter around his neck, trying to pull his head back down to hers.

He opened his mouth and covered hers, briefly licking the seam, end to end, tugging on her luscious full lips, before pulling away again. Her minty breath mingled with his and he groaned huskily and spoke against her mouth.

"If we don't stop now, Emma, I don't think I can. And as much as I want to pick you up and do all kinds of carnal things to this sexy body of yours—" He stopped, drawing in a deep breath. "I don't want you to think I'm trying to manipulate you, trying to—" He closed his eyes. "I just don't want to screw this up. I—"

When she placed a hand over his lips, his eyes opened to see her staring up at him.

"You're not manipulating me. I know exactly what I'm doing. I know exactly what I want."

He drew in a harsh breath when her small hand reached between their bodies to stroke the front of his pants, cupping his bulge through the thick fabric of his jeans.

"And what I want is you. Now."

Shane knew there was no way in hell he could walk away from her. He'd tried chivalry. He had tried dropping her off back at her place alone. Hell, he had even just tried to give Emma another chance to call it quits before this whole thing got started. But she didn't, and they were both in for a long night.

Chapter 12

As she stared up at him, the lids of her eyes were low and sultry while her focused fingers molded themselves around his shaft. His gaze was drawn to her lips, full, red and swollen from his kisses, begging for him to touch them, to kiss her until their gasps were so intertwined that they breathed as one.

Growing uncomfortably thick in his jeans, Shane knew if he didn't get away from her soon he'd have her on the bed, spread out, with him between her legs in two seconds flat.

"Are you sure?" he asked, and held his breath.

When he felt her nod of assent, he wasted no time. After quickly removing his jeans and shirt, throwing them on the floor next to the bed, he lifted her in his arms. Carrying her the short distance, he lowered her on the bed before gently letting her down, covering her body with his.

He placed his hands on either side of her face, lowered his mouth and kissed her, groaning when her tongue eagerly reached out to meet his, inviting him inside.

Emma moaned into his mouth her body on fire, as he ground against her, the tip of his naked shaft hot and hard against her thigh. She ground right back against him, welcoming him, wrapping her arms around him and pulling him even closer.

When she felt a dewy, sticky moisture on her thigh, a measure of sanity prevailed, and she placed her hand against his chest.

"What?" he asked huskily, running his mouth along her jaw.

She groaned when his tongue snaked out and licked the area his lips had caressed. But again she placed a restraining hand against his chest, moving him away.

"Protection…" She blew out a frustrated breath. She wanted him as badly as he wanted her. But she couldn't make love to him without protection.

"I—I'm sorry Shane. But, I can't. Not without—" Her words were cut off by his lips on hers. He pulled away, a sheepish look on his face.

"It's okay. God, I can't believe I almost forgot."

Shane couldn't believe he'd been seconds away from pushing into her, with no thought to her protection.

Not once—from the time he'd even been sexually involved with a woman until now—had that *ever* happened. Damn…he'd think about the significance of that later.

Right now, he needed to take care of her so they could pick up where they left off.

He moved away, snatching his jeans from the floor near the bed. He removed the foil-wrapped package and tossed the jeans to the side, ripping into the foil with his teeth and glancing over at her.

For a quick second he paused, wondering what she thought of him, condom in his wallet, as though this were something he did regularly. He was by no means a saint, yet he was discriminate in who he had sex with. He didn't have to wonder long, because soon Emma's hand reached out, covering both his hand and his erection. He paused, glancing over at her.

"Let me," she said, using her soft hand to gently push his away, taking over the job for him.

Emma lay on the bed, her body tingling, needy, on fire, wanting…needing to feel him back on her, covering her with his body. He'd made short work out of removing his clothes; jeans dispatched swiftly, shirt pulled over his head, shoes kicked off, and she had gasped when he turned, showing her what he was working with.

She'd suspected he was well endowed. She could tell from the hint of bulge discernible beneath his workout clothes. But dear God. She had no idea he would be this…beautiful.

His shaft resembled a perfectly sculpted piece of art. Smooth, the color was a shade darker than the rest of his body. Such a beautiful piece of masculinity.

She drew in a shaky breath.

It was so beautiful she needed to touch it. Had to touch it. Had to know what it felt like beneath her hands. Outline it with her fingers…

She pushed up onto her knees on the bed, and his surprised eyes met hers.

Emma pulled her bottom lip between her teeth as she pushed his hand away. Taking the condom away from him, she placed it on the bed beside her and grasped his penis.

He drew in a shuddering breath when her fingers brushed over him, feathering along the thick, dark vein that ran beneath his shaft, from the top of the smooth mushroom head to the stem and back again.

She wiped away a dewy bead from the tip with the pad of a finger. She glanced up at him from beneath lowered lashes, a small smile tipping the edges of her lips up as she noted the fine tremor of his hands, clenched at his sides.

She circled the thick length between her fingers, scoring his shaft before carefully grasping his heavy sac that hung like ripe plums behind his shaft.

When he groaned, she raised her eyes to meet his.

"God, Emma…baby…if you keep touching me like that, this won't last long," the words sounded strangled coming from his throat.

She grinned, allowing the heavy orbs to fall from her hand, lifting the condom from the bed beside her.

"May I?" she asked, raising her eyes to meet his. When he groaned this time, she laughed lightly, enjoying the way her touch affected him.

* * *

When she raised her soulful brown eyes to meet his, the look in them was a heady combination of innocence and seduction, and he nearly came on the spot. Every nerve ending was on fire, his body trembling with her innocent, hot touch. It only increased as he watched Emma pick up the condom beside her and remove it from the package.

In one smooth move she rolled it over his straining erection and lowered herself back down on the bed.

He rubbed the tip of his shaft back and forth between the lips of her moist folds. Her skin was soft, silky. Feminine perfection.

She drew in a gasping breath, her body arching off the bed with his playful swipes between her sensitive lips.

"Please…oh, please…" she moaned. The sweet sound of her cries rang out when he brought his mouth down to claim a breast.

Shane wanted, needed, to take his time with her. Needed to explore every inch of her decadent curves. Make love to every part of her.

He had to do whatever it took to end the feral need in him to claim her. Because once he claimed her, his fascination with her would end. At least that's what he told himself.

He drew a dark brown nipple deeply into his mouth, running his tongue over it before clamping his teeth down lightly.

"Shane…" she moaned again, this time her voice was sharp, piercing as she drew out his name. Her slightly husky voice echoed in the dark, quiet room and slid over his body like a warm silken caress.

The wet sound of her nipple smacking out of his mouth as he released her was hidden beneath the sound of her mewling cries as he inserted a finger inside her heat, testing her readiness.

He added another finger, stretching her slowly. He barely held back the need to spread her legs wide and push into her warmth when her walls tightened on his finger, clamping down.

Withdrawing her moisture, he brought it to his mouth. Keeping his eyes on hers, he licked his finger clean of her essence. Her eyes glittered with a wildness that mirrored his need.

It was time to end the tension that had been brewing between them. He inhaled deeply, taking in her unique smell, which tangled with his senses and made him go rock hard, from zero to a hundred miles in two seconds flat.

"Are you ready?" he asked, whispering the words against the corner of her mouth.

Emma went weak at the knees. She felt her own essence run down the side of her legs when his warm breath moved from her mouth to trail along the side of her neck, the slightly scratchy feel of his day beard setting off a sizzling, achy sensation along her body.

She was so ready that she was delirious.

"Mmm," she moaned, arching her body off the bed and gasping when he nosed the side her neck and nuzzled the sensitive skin directly beneath her earlobe. "Yes…"

The lids of her eyes drooped low as he grasped both of her wrists within one of his big hands and brought her arms up, above her head, causing her breasts to press against each other.

"Keep your hands, there. Don't move them," he instructed, and she bit the inside of her cheek to keep from screaming out.

He snaked down her body, grasped each of her thighs, and moments later his mouth touched the inside of her leg, nibbling the sensitive inner skin.

Butterflies fluttered violently in her stomach as she shut her eyes tightly and squirmed on the bed. He gently pushed her legs apart when she tried to clamp them together, her action an instinctual feminine defensive move against what he was making her feel.

"Oh, God, Shane," she moaned, her breath coming out in hitched puffs of air. She felt his rumbling, low laugh against her inner thigh.

Licking and biting his way along one thigh, only to turn to the other, giving it equal, sweet, decadent attention, the slightly rough skin of his cheek rubbed against her mound, back and forth in a see-sawing motion. Seconds later, he parted the lips of her vagina, and his tongue snaked out to stroke between her moist folds. The kiss was hot, dangerous and lethal.

With mind-blowing precision, he catered to her, licking and suckling, ferreting out the small nub of her clitoris and pulling it into his mouth.

Emma's head tossed back and forth on the pillow,

her body on fire with need. Ignoring his edict to keep her hands above her, she reached down to grasp his head.

Tunneling her hands through his silky strands, she pulled him closer, her body moving in sensual rhythm to the strokes of his talented tongue.

She felt her orgasm unfurl. Snaking though her body, a tingling sensation started in her toes and worked through her body, coiling though her senses before detonating.

The explosion was as intense as it was unexpected.

Emma shouted out loudly. No longer caring if anyone could hear them, she screamed her release, grinding her body against his mouth as he continued his sensual assault against her body.

Head thrown back, muscles straining, taut, on fire, her body arched sharply off the bed as she allowed the orgasm to wash over her.

He pushed her legs up so that her feet were planted on the bed, with him lying between her spread thighs. He grasped her hips, his fingers digging into their fleshy skin.

"Look at me." His voice was layered with lust, need and wild desire.

When she glanced up and met his eyes at the sensual command, she felt the broad head of his shaft at her entry.

Licking her lips, her eyes trailed over his face.

Her glance moved down the flaring at the ends of his nostrils, to the tightness of his jaw as though he were holding back, waiting, his eyes darkened with lust.

"Now…I need you now."

With her heartbeat thudding erratically in her chest, Emma gave him the permission he was waiting for.

Her breath came out in a long hiss when he began to enter her body.

Slowly, inch by decadent inch, he pushed into her, covering her body and claiming her mouth, pressing his tongue inside, deep.

Emma moaned against his mouth, squirmed beneath his body, trying desperately to adjust to his thickness; his unyielding invasion. One part of her felt trapped beneath him, afraid, like a wild animal caught, as he continued to feed her more of himself, stretching her so wide she felt every hot, torrid, unrelenting inch of him as he pressed deep inside her.

He cupped her buttocks and lifted her tighter against his body, swallowing her cry within the warmth of his mouth.

When he broke the kiss, he trailed his mouth over her face, until he reached her neck, licking the sensitive spot directly behind her ear.

"Emma…Emma!" Repositioning them, smoothly in one move, she straddled him, her legs on either side of his hips.

"I've wanted to feel you like this…" His hips rotated in slow, sure strokes deep within her, and Emma drew in a swift breath, clutching at his wide forearms to brace herself for the ride.

"To see you like this…" Another deep stroke and stars exploded behind her tightly closed lids.

The bed practically vibrated, and she opened her

eyes to see he'd lifted his torso into an upright position, their bodies in complete alignment. He palmed the back of her head, bringing her face closer to his, and immediately nuzzled the side of her neck.

"Since the moment we met…" His voice was barely more than a growl against her neck. His tongue swiped out to lick a hot path along her collarbone. "You taste so good. Feel so good…so damn good."

"Yes…"

She turned into his caress, her body adjusting to his. The strain from his entry now easing, they established a smooth, easy rhythm

"You, too. You feel…you feel so good…so good," she chanted over and over in panting breaths and broken sentences, barely able to speak, much less form coherent words.

As Shane moved inside her, he couldn't get close enough. It seemed like an eternity that he'd wanted to feel her, to taste her.

As he made love to her, every movement of her body, every moan she uttered made him want to beat his chest and go caveman on her, let the world know that it was he who had made her feel this good.

He gritted his teeth together, biting back the need to flip her on her back, to ride her harder until they both exploded.

As she grew comfortable to his girth, her legs widened, giving him easier access to her body. Gliding her body up and down along his shaft, riding him nice and slow, she made love to him in a way no one woman ever had before.

Shane prided himself on his longevity. Easily out-lasting lovers in the past, he always made sure their pleasure came before he took his own, but he wasn't sure he could do that this time. Not with Emma.

As her hips rolled against his, their bodies in perfect harmony, he placed his hands along her bouncing bottom and grunted. "I don't know how long I can last, baby…you fit me so snug—so damn perfect."

He heard her breathless laugh before she replied, "Good, because I feel the same way."

Several more thrusts into her warm sheath, her soft belly brushing against his with every bounce and glide, and he felt his groin tingle, and knew his release was seconds away.

He pulled away from her and flipped her on her back, eliciting a surprised groan from her, her passion-glazed eyes staring up at him.

He ran a glance over her plush, red lips.

"God…please tell me you're ready…"

"Yes," she moaned.

With a groan, Shane placed an arm around her slim waist, anchoring her to his body tighter. He wrapped his other arm around her neck, holding her steady as he pumped inside of her.

One, two, three more deep-seated strokes and he exploded. Rocking into her a final time, they both gave in to the mind-blowing release.

Chapter 13

Emma's head lay on Shane's chest, her petite body spooned against his much larger one. One big leg lay crosswise over both of hers, effectively securing her within his embrace.

The early morning light peeked through the slits of her blinds, allowing the dawn to filter into the room as Emma pried her eyes open.

Arching her back, she winced, biting the corner of her mouth.

She couldn't believe what she'd experienced with Shane last night. She glanced down at him.

His face was turned away from hers as his head rested on the pillow. In profile, she could make out the shadow of his overnight beard.

She turned away from him, glancing down at her

body. Easing a hand between them, she brushed her fingers over the skin of her inner thighs. A hot blush blossomed on her cheeks instantly as she remembered the feel of his stubble against the sensitive skin on her inner thigh as he'd made love to her in the most intimate way, more than once during their marathon lovemaking session.

She glanced at the small alarm clock on her dresser, surprised when she realized how late it was. It was nearly six-thirty, an hour past the time she normally rose.

Realizing it was Saturday, she relaxed and settled back against him.

"I wasn't too much for you, was I?"

Startled, Emma glanced away from the clock and down at the man whose body was wrapped intimately around hers.

"Hey…I didn't know you were awake," she replied, her voice hoarse. Again, she felt her cheeks flush. The state of her voice was due to the cries he'd wrung from her throughout the long night.

She willingly allowed him to pull her back, her bottom nestled firmly against his groin. She drew in a surprised breath, feeling his shaft, laying thick, erect and long against her backside.

"No," she whispered, answering his question. "It wasn't too much," she finished simply. She laughed at her understatement. The way he'd made love to her, the way he'd made her feel as he'd catered to every inch of her body, sent a curl of remembered deliciousness racing through her body.

We'd like to send you two free books to introduce you to Kimani™ Romance books. These novels feature strong, sexy women, and African-American heroes that are charming, loving and true. Our authors fill each page with exceptional dialogue, exciting plot twists, and enough sizzling romance to keep you riveted until the very end!

KIMANI ROMANCE...LOVE'S ULTIMATE DESTINATION

Your two books have a combined cover price of $13.98, but are yours **FREE!**

We'll even send you two wonderful surprise gifts. You can't lose!

THE EDITOR'S "THANK YOU" FREE GIFTS INCLUDE:

Two Kimani™ Romance Novels
Two exciting surprise gifts

YES! I have placed my Editor's "thank you" Free Gifts seal in the space provided at right. Please send me 2 FREE books, and my 2 FREE Mystery Gifts. I understand that I am under no obligation to purchase anything further, as explained on the back of this card.

PLACE FREE GIFTS SEAL HERE

About how many NEW paperback fiction books have you purchased in the past 3 months?

❏ 0-2   ❏ 3-6   ❏ 7 or more
E7XY   E5MH   E5MT

168/368 XDL

Please Print

FIRST NAME

LAST NAME

ADDRESS

APT.#   CITY

STATE/PROV.   ZIP/POSTAL CODE

Thank You!

BUSINESS REPLY MAIL
FIRST-CLASS MAIL   PERMIT NO. 717   BUFFALO, NY

POSTAGE WILL BE PAID BY ADDRESSEE

THE READER SERVICE
PO BOX 1867
BUFFALO NY 14240-9952

NO POSTAGE
NECESSARY
IF MAILED
IN THE
UNITED STATES

"No one has ever made me feel like that before. So alive. So beautiful. So wanted. So needed." She boldly made the admission, holding her breath waiting for his reaction.

She felt the tension ease from his body.

He laughed low, a sexy rumble against the back of her neck that sent a sizzle of heat directly to the core of her. She moved her legs when his big fingers trailed down her stomach and cupped her mound.

"Good," he murmured. "Because I feel the same way."

Her body arched away from his talented fingers before she placed a steady hand over his. "But I think I need to take a long, hot herbal bath…alone, before round two."

"Round two?"

She blushed again, remembering how many times throughout the long night and early morning hours they'd made love.

There was contented silence between them. Emma, beyond exhausted, stifled a yawn as she felt her eyelids drooping. Seconds before she was about to give in to her exhaustion and doze off again, he spoke.

"It seems like I've been taking care of myself my whole life."

The switch in topic brought her to full wakefulness.

Although it was a part of her job as a journalist, as well as in her very nature to be curious, she was intensely private about her own life. She recognized that same trait in Shane. That he was, once again, candidly sharing a part of his past with her both surprised and thrilled her.

"You mentioned being brought up in a group home."

She felt his kiss on the back of her head, before he pulled away and sighed.

"Yeah. I was twelve when I was placed in foster care."

"That must have been difficult."

He laughed without humor. "It was. When my mother...died." Again he hesitated before mentioning his mother's death, just as he had in the club.

She attributed the hesitation to it being something difficult for him to say, unconsciously running the tips of her fingers along his forearms in a soothing manner.

"What happened to your father?"

"He took off, not long after I was born. I never knew him. It had always been just me and mom. In foster care I felt alone for the first time in my life. Left alone without anyone giving a damn what happened to me, one way or another."

Emma drew in a deep breath at the revelation. Thinking of her own life, she realized how much she identified with him.

"What about you?"

She snuggled back, deeper into his arms, biting at the corner of mouth, hesitating, still thinking over what he'd shared with her when he spoke. She tucked the revelations away to examine further. He nuzzled the side of her neck, kissing her in the sensitive spot beneath the lobe of her ear, making goose bumps settle down her arms.

"What's your story, Emogene, aka Gene, Rawlings?" he probed again, and Emma heard the humor tinged with curiosity in his voice.

"My parents were real adventurers," she finally said and smiled a bittersweet smile, thinking of her parents. "They met in college, were both liberal arts majors. They wanted to make a difference in the world, they told me. They also believed in experiencing life to the fullest, which is just a fancy way of saying we never stayed in one place for too long."

"Is that where you got your love for traveling…your parents?"

Emma considered his question before answering.

It was true, traveling to unique places, discovering unique cultures and new adventures had always seemed to beckon her. But she had always thought she had the same wanderlust as everyone else, but she just decided to act on it. The joy of discovering new things had been one of the most pleasurable aspects of her career, yet, just like her parents, she'd eventually grow restless if she were in one place too long.

Recently, though, the novelty had begun to wear thin. Being on the road was constantly losing some of its appeal, and she thought of settling down, maybe writing a book on the various cultures she'd learned about. But whenever the thought came she dismissed it, never able to envision choosing one place she could permanently call home.

"Maybe. At least, that's one part of it."

"And the other?"

Emma grew uncomfortable with his probing questions. Not that they were too personal, but because they forced her to examine things she normally left in the back of her mind, buried deep. Forced her to examine the reasons she grew restless yet couldn't imagine settling down. The thought of being alone scared her more than she was ready to admit to herself.

"My parents died in a plane crash, and I was shuttled back and forth between relatives," she began haltingly. "I never stayed long enough to grow any attachment to any of them." She shrugged one shoulder in feigned nonchalance. "No one really wanted me around anyway…so I guess it was no one's loss when I moved on."

Her low-spoken words zeroed in on Shane's heart like a well-aimed bullet, straight and direct. Shane brought her close to his body and listened as she, hesitantly at first, spoke of her childhood. He was as silent as she'd been when he'd opened up to her. Something he rarely did with anyone. The reasons he felt comfortable with her were reasons he didn't understand himself.

He'd had no intention of spending the morning with her. He'd thought he could just make love to her and get her out of his system. Something he told himself was all that he needed.

But after the first time, he knew it wasn't enough. He didn't know how or when it would be enough.

Damn. He was falling for her.

He didn't know how it happened, when or why. An

inner voice mocked him. He knew exactly when it had begun. It had been from the first time he'd seen her climbing the rappelling wall, followed up by the way she stood up to him in Roebuck's office, her determined little chin lifted, daring him to try to get rid of her.

He played the role of the carefree bachelor to a fault. He'd never had a need for anything beyond the physical with any of the women he'd been with in the past. And if he occasionally found something lacking in his relationships, or thought maybe he wanted more, something would happen to disabuse him of the notion.

The last time he'd felt something more than casual lust for a woman had been for Ciara, and after that, well, everything had changed for him.

He ran an absent hand over her soft hair, trailing his fingers down her body.

With Emma, his normal mode of operating had been thrown right out the window, and he hadn't a clue in hell how to retrieve it. He wasn't sure that he wanted to, even if he knew how.

Beyond the normal pillow talk he had engaged in with partners of the past, saying things he knew they wanted to hear just to make them feel good, with Emma he went deeper, said things he rarely disclosed. And it felt good to do it. As they lay there, spooned together, it felt natural being with her like this as she shared stories of her life as a journalist, at times laughing along with her at the more humorous tales, and sharing her remorse when hearing of the more heartrending stories.

Like two saddle-shy wild horses, they were beginning

to warm to the idea of inviting another into their lives, both gradually giving guarded secrets of themselves to the other.

But Shane was hungry for more. He found himself really wanting to know who she was, beyond the superficial.

He recalled a time when Kyle had laughed at him, warning him that when love hit, it hit hard and unexpectedly and there was nothing a man could do about it, but give in and enjoy the ride.

Love.

Damn.

The minute he thought it, he was brought up short mentally.

There was no way was he falling in love with her. It wasn't possible. Whatever it was he felt for her, whatever they had going…could never last.

Even as he was having the one-sided mind fight, Shane rubbed his cheek against her hair, breathing in her unique scent deeply as he ran his hand over the soft skin of her stomach in an unconscious, soothing gesture.

He shook his head, as though to rid himself of the notion that he could be falling for her.

"With the way I was brought up, never having a real home I guess, I suppose it was a natural career choice for me, being a journalist."

"I guess living that way would do that for anyone," he murmured.

"Yes, I suppose so. I never felt as though I…" she said, pausing "…fit, I guess, is as good a word as any. I always felt like I was on the outside looking in. The whole 'square peg trying to fit in a round hole' syndrome."

Shane felt the pain behind the casual words.

"I never felt like I was special in any way. It wasn't anyone's fault but mine, I guess. I just never…fit," she repeated, her voice going soft. When her words came to a halting stop, he pulled her around to face him, looking deeply into her eyes.

"What?" she asked, self-consciously running a hand over her hair. "I must look like a mess." She shifted as though to move away from him, and he tugged her back against his body.

"You're very special," he told her, removing his T-shirt that she'd donned, exposing her pretty breasts to his avid gaze.

"Every part of you." He reached out and captured one of her nipples, toying with it until it spiked against his fingers. "Inside and out."

She ducked her head, but not before he caught the hint of a smile and one deep dimple flash.

"And anyone, including me, who thinks otherwise is a damn fool."

She raised her head and looked at him, tilting it to the side, a question in her eyes. Before she could say a word, he lifted her, placing her body on top of his, and brought their bodies flush, taking her mouth with his.

After a long, hot kiss, he reluctantly released her.

"Do I make you feel good, Emma? Special?" He murmured the question against her mouth.

When he nosed down the length of her neck, she moved her head to the side to give him better access.

"Yes," she replied in a breathy whisper, laughing huskily. "You do."

"Good. Because I plan to make you feel so special you're too weak to walk straight."

She laughed outright at his lecherous claim.

With slow deliberation, he smoothly flipped their bodies so that he covered her and lowered his mouth, making good on his promise.

Emma woke with a smile stretching her mouth wide.

She turned, expecting to find a warm body next to her, but instead her groping hand grasped a piece of paper where Shane's head should have been.

Prying her eyes open, she dragged her body away from the mattress. She opened the paper, her eyes scanning over the short sentence written in a broad, masculine script.

Be ready at formation. No excuses, slacker. Even if you can't walk straight.

She grinned and placed the note on the nightstand before throwing her legs over the edge of the bed, her heart light as she grabbed her clothes and started to get ready for the day.

Chapter 14

The daylong rush of adrenaline was fading from Emma, exhaustion finally creeping up on her as she dragged herself inside the station.

And if Emma had been under the delusion that the intimacy she and Shane had shared, or their mutual disclosures, would affect how he treated her during the day, she would have been sorely disappointed.

With a groan of relief, she plunked down into the first available chair she could find as soon as she entered the reception area.

In fact, if anything, he'd been more demanding. The day's activity had included yet another simulation, this one in a smoke-filled room where the rookies had five seconds to don gas masks and protective gear and find and drag out of the building three civilians, two adults and a child, which were made of canvas and sand to simulate the weight of each.

And of course he'd invited her to participate.

And of course she'd been unable to resist the challenge.

She felt a grin tug at the corners of her mouth. They were quite a pair.

"Tough day?"

With a start, she glanced up into the sympathetic smiling face of Belle. She slumped back into the chair.

"Yeah, you could say that," Emma replied, wrinkling her nose.

"This'll make you feel better."

When she noted the cup of steaming liquid the woman was holding out to her, she waved it away with a smile. "Thanks, Belle. But it might take me a minute to get up," she said with a groan. She placed her hands on the arms of the chair, preparing to push herself upright, when Belle waved a stalling hand.

"No, don't get up. I'll bring it to you," she said, coming from behind the counter. She ambled over and sat in the chair next to Emma, handing her the mug. "I made it from the herbs in my own garden. Chamomile, rosemary and a sprig of peppermint."

Emma brought the cup to her nose. "Smells great," she said gratefully before taking a cautious sip.

"I added a little honey as well. Nice and relaxing. Looks like you could use it."

"Boy, can I!" Emma took another drink, this one

longer, the hot liquid easing down her throat, and sighed.

"So, you and 'Mr. Hot Sex on a Platter' have been getting along pretty well, huh?"

The blunt question made Emma spew hot liquid from her mouth, her eyes opening fully.

"Oh, my God...what are you talking about?" she asked, accepting the napkin from the woman and wiping the dribble of tea from her chin before placing the mug carefully on the chipped round wood table near her chair.

The woman cast her a knowing look.

"Look, sweetie. I might be a little gray around the edges—" she ran a hand over her immaculate, upswept hair and winked at Emma "—but this old gal's not dead!"

Emma glanced around to see if anyone else had entered the area, overhearing the woman's words and cackling laugh.

"Oh, honey, take it easy...it's no big deal. Besides, it's not as though it's any big secret with the way you two have been carrying on! Besides, I knew it was coming the first time I saw the two of you together," the older woman said with a smug expression on her face.

"And that would be...?" she asked, the question trailing off as she looked into the woman's knowing eyes.

"That would be when you were walking around with your tail tucked beneath your butt, acting like you were afraid of your own doggone shadow around that man.

Not to mention the many, *many* times I caught Shane checking out your booty when he thought no one was watching."

Again, the old woman's blunt words almost made Emma choke.

"Calm down." Belle chuckled again. "You two haven't been *that* bad. But it's hard to hide when two people become involved. And I don't think you two could hide it, even if you tried." A faraway look entered her eyes. "That kind of passion is impossible to keep under wraps."

To buy herself time before answering, Emma asked, "Have we been that obvious? You know… unprofessional? Are the others talking about us?"

The last thing Emma wanted or needed was for her professionalism to come into question.

"No one's saying anything, no worries."

Emma blew out a relieved breath. "Thank God!"

After several moments, the two women drank their sweet tea in companionable silence.

"Well…have you?" Belle asked, returning to her question with the precision of a terrorist inquisitor.

So much for dodging the bullet, Emma thought.

She considered lying. But what was the point? She glanced over at the old woman calmly sipping her tea and felt a grin tugging at the corners of her mouth, before it blossomed into a full smile.

"Ummm, well…yes," she admitted, despite the heat she felt literally burning up her cheeks. "We have."

"Alrighty then, that's what I'm talking about!" Belle

replied, holding up her hand. Laughing outright, Emma slapped palms with the woman.

Emma had never really talked to other women. Not about personal issues at any rate. With her way of living, and her line of work, she'd never really had many "girlfriends." Even in college, she'd been so focused on school and work that she'd always been somewhat of a loner.

"Okay, so spill."

"I'm not sure that there's really much to talk about." Emma tucked a strand of hair back behind her ear that had escaped her "uniform" ponytail, feeling oddly shy.

She laughed at herself. Here she was at the age of twenty-eight, blushing over a guy as though she were a teenager.

"Sweetie, when the lovin' is good, there is absolutely *nothing* wrong with a woman blushing. Fact is, if a man don't make you blush, he ain't doing something right! That's when you have to worry!"

After their mutual laughter subsided, Emma turned to her, sobering, thinking of Shane and their new, albeit complex, relationship. She opened her mouth to ask a question and promptly shut it, not sure how to ask. Truth was, she didn't even know *what* to ask.

"It's been amazing. Especially the last couple of days with him." Emma paused, considering. "He's beginning to open up to me. He shared some of his own story, why he became a jumper. He doesn't seem to have a problem with me being here anymore."

"I would imagine not," Belle interjected.

"Yeah, well, I guess that's obvious." Emma smiled lightly before continuing. "But beyond *that,* he's been really helpful in other ways. Some of the things he's told me are personal as well. Things I would never have thought he'd share with me, he has." She paused. "I...I think he's beginning to trust me. I don't think he does that very easily."

What Emma told Belle was true, yet, for as open as he was to her, sharing stories, encouraging the others to speak to her, share their stories, there was a part of himself she felt he kept from her.

"Men are a funny breed. Remember that book about men being from Mars and women from... Oh, hell, where was it?" Belle asked, frowning.

"Venus?"

"Yep, that's the one. Well, for men like Shane, it even goes a step farther. They don't open up as easily. They don't show their feelings in the same way we do." She stopped and shook her head. "My Carl was a lot like Shane. He would jump into the most perilous situations. Hell, my man lived for it! But ask him to share his feelings and he'd as soon cut out his own tongue! They live a dangerous life, putting their lives on the line to protect and serve. Those type of men are the hardest ones to get to open up and tell you what they're really thinking."

"But when they do, sweetheart, when they allow you into their worlds, it's a beautiful thing. It's special. Not something that comes easily for them. And when they open their hearts and love...it's real. Deep. They love hard and long."

Had Shane loved someone who'd hurt him? Was that the reason for his initial distrust of her? The reason at times she felt his hesitance in opening up to her?

She was ready to ask the woman the questions burning in her mind when the door to the station opened and the man in question entered the room.

"Hey, I was looking for you," he said, the lines etched around his sensual mouth showing his fatigue. Yet the smile on his face, meant only for her, transformed it, softening it. Emma returned the soft smile, her eyes on his, momentarily forgetting Belle, who was watching the exchange between the two lovers.

He walked toward her, covered in soot. His face, jumpsuit and every exposed inch of skin was sooty, from the day of training in the mock blow-up site.

Emma felt a part of her chest tighten in response to the hero he was, while another part of her, the purely feminine part, melted for the man he was, the man behind the role of hero he played on a daily basis. And yet another part wondered how long this could actually last. She shook her head, determined not to dwell on those types of thoughts and just enjoy what they had for the moment.

He came to stand next to her and stopped. Emma glanced at his outstretched hand. Without hesitation, she placed her hand within his strong grasp and allowed him to pull her to her feet.

"Come home with me."

Neither one of them heard Belle's soft chuckle as he led her away.

Chapter 15

The aroma of bacon and the hum of a deep baritone singing off-key brought Emma from a sound sleep.

Yawning wide, she opened her eyes as Shane entered the bedroom, wearing nothing more than an apron around his lean waist and balancing a tray overloaded with food.

She narrowed her eyes and read the slogan on his apron as he approached the bed. In bold red letters were the words "Firemen like it HOT," and on a fireman's pole was a woman wearing a helmet and a pair of stilettos and carrying an ax.

And nothing else.

When he noticed her appraisal of the apron, he actually blushed, mumbling, "It was, uh, a gift."

She laughed outright at the almost boyish look of

chagrin on his face, but she decided to let him off and not ask who the gift was from.

He sat down, tray in hand, near her on the bed. "I thought you might be hungry," he said.

"Shane, there's enough here to feed an army!" she said, eyeing the array of food as she scooted over to make room for him on the bed.

"I thought you could use the energy, rebuild your strength."

She caught the twinkle in his eyes, groaning, remembering their marathon lovemaking session the night before.

Last night, after a side trip to her room, where he'd instructed her to pack for a weekend away from the station, they'd quickly rid themselves of their clothing, their desire for each other building to a slow boil, until it was ready to explode.

She hadn't had time to question his order to pack, much less do any actual packing, before he was on her.

Removing only the bare essential clothing before tumbling on the bed together, their lovemaking had been hot and fast, leaving them both temporarily sated and completely breathless.

She'd played with the heavy sprinkling of hair on his chest, twirling it around her finger, his chest pillowing her head.

"Pack for what?" she'd asked, once her heartbeat had returned to normal.

"I thought you'd like to get away from the station." As she toyed with his chest hair, he stroked a casual hand down her. "I thought we could take a trip to Sweetwater Gap, near Wind River Peak. That is, if you're interested?" he asked, looking down at her.

"It sounds like fun. I'd love to!"

"Great." He nodded. "I have a small house near downtown Lander. It's not much, but it's home. We can go there tonight. We'll wake up bright and early and drive down to the site. It's got a lot of history, and it's a great place to take some photos as well. I haven't been there since Kyle took me, right before I joined the smoke jumpers."

At the mention of his mentor, Emma had become more alert. He had rarely spoken of him, beyond mentioning him that first time, at the bar. Beyond that, she only knew that Shane considered Kyle his best friend and owed his life to him. The fact that he wanted to share it with her, a place that held special memories for him, with her hadn't escaped her attention.

By the time they'd reached his home, it had been late. After taking a quick shower together, they'd fallen into bed. Waking up hours later, he'd made slow, leisurely love to her that lasted throughout most of the night.

"This looks amazing. Please tell me you ordered out for this!" she said, and he laughed, picking up one of the plump strawberries from the platter and dipping it into the saucer of cream.

She dutifully opened her mouth, allowing him to pop the strawberry inside. Closing her eyes she moaned. "Mmm…delicious."

"Nope. I made it myself." Her eyes sprang open when she felt his mouth cover her chin, his tongue sweep out and lick away the dollop of cream and strawberry juice that had eased from her mouth.

When his wicked tongue licked a path up her chin to her mouth, Emma opened wide and met his tongue with hers.

When Shane felt her stomach rumble against his chest, he reluctantly drew away from her.

"Guess I know which hunger we have to take care of first," he quipped, and smiled when she wrinkled her nose at him. "Besides, we have to leave soon for Sweetwater."

"How far is it from here?" she asked around the bacon she was chewing.

He leaned back against the headboard and swiped a piece of toast from her hand right before she could take a bite, dodging the swat of her hand.

"Hey, get your own!" she groused as he crunched down on the toast in satisfaction.

"It's about a two-hour trip to the actual site, not including the hike to the Wind River Peak. We'll pack a lunch and gear. Wait…I didn't even think to ask you. Do you like camping?"

"I've done my fair share."

"Good, we'll take camping gear as well."

He settled beside her and this time took food from the platter, instead of stealing from her plate, after she cast a playfully evil look his way.

"Sounds like fun. So besides the photo op for me, what's special about this place?"

She turned to him. The answering smile slid from her face when she noticed the look on his.

"I'll tell you all about it on the way." He finally answered. "Sound fair?"

"Okay. Sounds fair," she replied, tucking away her curiosity. They made quick work of the food, and before she knew it nothing remained but scraps.

She laughed. "I guess I was hungry."

"Me, too. But now I'm hungry for you."

He pushed the tray away and planted a kiss on her mouth.

"I thought you said we didn't have time to *indulge* in those hungers right now."

"There's always time for a little indulging, Emma. Always," he replied, before capturing her mouth with his.

Chapter 16

Dry air blew warmly across Emma's face as she peered through the lens of her Nikon.

She angled the camera toward the billowing clouds and took several shots before refocusing so that the majestic-looking Wind River Mountains were brought into tighter view.

Beyond the few scattered ranches they encountered on the way to Sweetwater and the occasional convenience store/gas station peppered along the endless stretch of country highway, the route could have appeared as the set of a movie depicting the end of civilization.

They'd stopped only once to refuel at one of the rare stations they encountered before they drove over the last pass that would take them into Lander Cutoff. From there it was another twenty miles until they reached their destination.

"We'll be there in ten minutes."

Emma leaned against the seat and smiled over at Shane. Despite the long drive, Emma couldn't deny the appeal of being alone with Shane.

And she loved the other side of his personality, one she'd glimpsed only occasionally. The carefree boyish side, where he'd do anything and everything to make her giggle. And one of those had been his driver's side karaoke rendition of an old Ike and Tina Turner song.

When the song had come on the radio, Emma reached forward and turned up the volume, dancing lightly in her seat, feeling carefree and just…happy, happier than she'd felt in a long time.

When he'd started singing along, complete with falsetto, Emma had laughed until her side ached. "Your voice is higher than Tina's!"

"Yeah, well, you have to admit, I do a damn good falsetto!"

"Oh yeah, you're good, all right," she'd quipped back.

When he wriggled his brows up and down, Emma shook her head, completely enjoying their exchange and enthralled with this side of him, one she was beginning to see was yet another part of the complex man that he was.

"If you ever want to think about a new career, I think you should seriously look into doing a karaoke tour. You're a natural!" She smirked as he pinned her with a mock glare.

"I'll have you know I'm known as the karaoke king of Lander," he said, one side of his mouth quirking in a smile he was trying to hide from her.

"You are not!"

"Am, too! I take my karaoke seriously. In fact, I'm thinking of taking my act on the road after the fire season is over," he said, totally deadpan. If not for the glimmer of humor in his light blue eyes, Emma would have sworn he was serious.

"Oh, God, you need help!" she replied, dissolving into giggles.

Emma brought her camera from her lap. Instead of bringing the lens to her eye, she simply observed the landscape unfolding. Throughout the drive, she'd been struck at times by the desolation of the area. Although she'd traveled extensively in her profession, usually in remote locations, at the moment she couldn't recall another place where she'd felt so completely cut off from the world. Ordinarily the feeling of being alone was as familiar as it was comfortable for Emma. She'd felt alone for most of her life.

She turned and glanced over at Shane. A small smile played around his sensual mouth as he tapped his fingers on the steering wheel in time to the music from the radio.

As though aware of her thoughts, he turned his attention from the road briefly, his thick eyebrows lifting in question.

She shook her head, silently reassuring him that everything was fine.

When he returned his attention to the road, she immediately amended her thoughts.

Despite the isolation of the area, she *didn't* feel cut off or alone. And that was because of Shane. The realization came at the same time as another one hit, and this one made her draw in a shuddering breath.

She blew out the air slowly, her heart racing as she glanced down at her hands.

Her fingers were clutching her camera, her arms trembling from the tension of her grip. She forced them to relax, breathing in and out in even breaths to try to combat the dizzy feeling that was making her head spin and her stomach roll.

She allowed herself to lay against the headrest as she closed her eyes.

She was falling in love with him.

"You okay?"

"Yes…I'm fine," she replied after several moments, and cleared her throat. She kept her eyes closed, unable to look at him, the reality of her feelings slamming into her, hard and unexpected.

"Just resting my eyes for a minute."

"Okay. But don't rest too long. We'll be there in another few minutes or so."

She cleared her throat, forcing words through lips gone dry. "Great." When she felt the dizziness pass, she glanced over at him. The lines of his forehead creased, concern in his eyes.

"You sure you're okay?"

She made herself nod, past the melon-sized lump

rolling around in her stomach. She turned away from him, staring out the window, lost in her own thoughts.

"Ohhhh, Shane…"

Shane paused in his unpacking, shielding his eyes from the sun's glare as he glanced up at her, the look of rapture on her face tugging a grin from him.

"Should I be jealous?"

She laughed lightly but didn't respond, too busy taking a rapid-fire succession of pictures.

She all but vibrated with excitement.

Shane stopped unpacking, unable to look away from her.

They were headed toward the southern end of Wind River Range, which would lead them to the remote Sweetwater Trailhead. After setting up camp, he planned for them to hike to Wind River Peak early in the morning, before he'd take her to the site itself.

After he'd found a good spot to set up camp for the night, he'd brought out their gear, and as he worked getting them set up, she roamed the area, taking shot after shot.

As he watched, she alternated between snapping off shots and glancing over the landscape, occasionally looking down at her camera and checking the images she captured. Once satisfied with what she had, she brought the camera back to her eyes and took more pictures.

Sitting back on his haunches, he allowed his gaze to rake over her, relieved that whatever happened in the truck to dispel their lighthearted banter and make her go silent on him had gone away, recalling the change that had come over her during the last ten minutes of their drive to their base camp.

When he'd asked her to come to Sweetwater, he'd asked her for a few reasons. The first was to help her with her article, thinking the opportunity for her to learn about the site and take pictures would be invaluable to her.

The second reason had been less noble, which was to simply be alone with her without having to share her attention with the others, a time for just the two of them. The third was one he was still struggling with.

He hadn't brought anyone to Sweetwater. And the fact that he wanted to bring Emma further into his world, on a more private level, in a way he'd not shared with anyone else, lurked in the back of his mind.

"It's absolutely beautiful, Shane," she said with near reverence in her voice, finally turning around to face him.

"You're a nature lover, are you?"

"Without a doubt!" She grinned at him, before bringing the camera back to her eyes and taking a flurry of shots.

In her excitement, her chest swayed just the smallest bit, jostling beneath the T-shirt she wore as she moved around, angling her camera toward whatever it was that had caught her eye.

After taking a few more shots, she released the camera and allowed it to hang from the strap suspended around her neck.

"Got enough for now?"

"Yep, I think I have enough." It was then that she glanced at the site, noticing the work he'd done. "Oh, Shane, I'm sorry! I didn't mean to get caught up in work. I should have helped."

He stood, dusting his palms against his khakis, smiling down at her. "It's no problem. I enjoyed watching you."

"So what's on the agenda?" she asked as he walked toward her, her face glowing.

"You know, I like this side of you," he said, pulling her into his arms.

When he wrapped his arms around her, holding her loosely within his grip she immediately lifted her arms around his neck.

"Oh, yeah? And what side is that?"

"I don't know…laid-back, content." He shrugged. "Carefree. I don't think I've seen this side of you. I like it," he finished simply. She tilted her head to the side, considering him, a grin on her face.

"There are many sides to me, Shane Westwood, and don't you forget it. I'm a complex woman, didn't ya know?" she quipped, and he kissed the tip of her round nose and pulled away.

"Yes, I'm beginning to see that." He smiled down at her.

Devoid of makeup, her thick hair secured in a high ponytail, her lips, pouty and full, smiling up at him, Shane was struck with her natural beauty.

When she stood there, within his arms, gazing up at him, only a hint of a smile on her face, Shane felt his heart ricochet inside his chest, as the reality of what he felt for her hit him like the proverbial ton of bricks.

He noticed the ghost of a smile slip from her face. He must have stared too long.

He moved one hand away from her waist and skimmed it up the length of her back before reaching her neck.

Her gaze remained glued to his, as he trailed his fingertips around until he reached her slender neck, spanning the hollow of her throat with his outstretched hand.

Right there, he wanted to lay her down and make love to her. Make love until the two of them were too weak to do anything but lay useless and weak. Make love to her until there was no memory of anyone else for either of them. Make love to her until neither one of them could deny what was happening to them. Make love to her until he could forget the reasons he felt more comfortable being alone and didn't buy into the notion of happily ever after with a woman. He immediately rejected the thought. What they had was hot, amazing. The sex was the most explosive he'd ever shared with someone else. But that's all it was, all it could ever be, even if sometimes his heart told him otherwise.

He rested his forehead against hers briefly before easing away.

"We'd better get a move on, while there's still light."

Chapter 17

Emma grimaced and readjusted her pack.

Her feet hurt like hell and her back was beginning to burn from carrying the backpack for the last hour. Although Shane had carried the heavier pack with most of their gear, she was more than ready to take a break.

Despite that, she pressed on, excited for the opportunity to view a historical fire and gather information for her article. But more than that, she was eager and more than a bit anxious, wondering what it was about the place they were headed that held significance for Shane. And she was more than sure that it did hold some value for him.

"Just over this bridge is the trail that will lead to the

site," he told her as she was hoisting the pack higher on her back.

"Want me to take that for you?" he asked, with concern in his eyes as he looked down at her while she readjusted the backpack.

"I got it," she replied, smiling past her fatigue, trudging on as they continued along the path.

When it dropped quickly, ending at a long, roped-off bridge set above a small creek, Shane turned back around to face her. "We're almost there. There it is, over there," he said, pointing.

Just beyond the bridge, where he was pointing, she spotted a clearing that would take them to their final site.

After crossing the old, wooden bridge, Emma kept glancing over at Shane, feeling the tension shrouding him grow thicker the closer they got. When they finally reached the site, Emma drew in a deep breath, a strange sadness overwhelming her. Unlike the land along the path leading up to the site, this area was barren, with its straw-colored grass and hollowed-out remnants of trees, all of which were evidence of the extremity of the fire's devastation long ago.

Oddly burdened, Emma allowed her pack to drop to her feet, and with a heavy heart lifted her camera to take several shots.

She didn't know Shane had come up behind her until he spoke. "Over there is the cabin that still stands. The only one that survived the fire. Come on, I'll take you over there."

Placing her camera back in her backpack, she

followed him the short distance to the burned-out cabin.

Shane removed their gear from his back, placing it near the rotted steps, and turned to Emma.

"This was the first place that Kyle took me, right after I passed the test, the day after I became a jumper," he began. Although he was looking down at her, it was as though he wasn't really seeing her.

He turned away, looking off to the distance. "The fire grew fast. It was so fast that the West Yellowstone jumpers had to call in reinforcements."

Emma's brow wrinkled. She knew the story. And because of the dates, she wondered about the significance for Shane and his friend, both having been too young to actually have jumped the fire.

He turned to face her again, seemingly guessing her thoughts from her expression. "No, he didn't jump it, but it was there that he became a man, he told me. Come here," he said, reaching out for her to take his hand.

He sat down on the feeble steps to the old cabin, stretching his long legs out in front of him, and Emma followed, sitting close, turning toward him.

"Kyle came from a long line of firefighters and smoke jumpers. His grandfather was one of the first smoke jumpers in the West, in Montana. Kyle's father belonged to the first group of men to start the station here in Wyoming. This was the last fire his father jumped. And he was here to witness it."

"Oh, Shane…I'm sorry for your friend."

Emma leaned into his body, sympathetic to the sadness and remorse in his voice for his friend's loss.

Shane glanced down, offering her an absent smile. "It was hard for Kyle. He was only ten at the time, and it was the first time he'd managed to convince his father to watch him jump. His father's chute didn't open correctly, and the secondary one came out late and the wind had changed direction and blew him into a burning tree. The jump line wrapped around his body, and he couldn't cut it before it was too late. Kyle witnessed the entire thing."

"Oh, God, that's awful!"

Shane sighed. "Yeah, it was. His father was everything to him." He turned to face her, and she wrapped both arms around his waist.

"When Kyle brought me here, it wasn't to share a sad story. It was to tell me that this was the place where he became a man."

"How so?"

"They'd gotten his father down, and after air-evacuating him out, he lived long enough to say goodbye to both Kyle and his mother. Kyle made his father a promise that he would do the same thing his father did, the same thing as his grandfather. He promised to protect those who needed him."

Emma remained silent, her arms still linked around his waist as he spoke.

"Part of that promise was to continue their family's dedication to fighting fires. The other was to take care of his mother.

"He knew my own story, but Kyle was never one to

preach. He never was one to tell a man how to *be* a man. He led by example. Both as a man and a jumper."

Emma held her breath, feeling the tension in his body.

"See, I never thought I had been man enough for my own mother. After my father left, my mother had to work two jobs, and in between those times, I rarely saw her."

He stopped, drawing in a breath. "And when I did, nine times out of ten she had a glass of scotch in one hand and no time for me. I hated her. I hated her for bailing out on me like that. I hated her for a lot of reasons."

He stopped talking. Emma wondered what it must have been like for him, her heart aching for the boy he once was.

"I started getting in trouble. A lot. Guess I thought bad attention was better than no attention at all. Skipping school, stealing…" He stopped, and Emma nodded, remembering when he told her the first night they were together about the trouble he got into as a young man. She hadn't known at the time it had started earlier in his childhood, believing his behavior started when he was in foster care.

"Eventually my trouble got the attention of the school social worker, and the state took over. They placed me in foster care after coming out for a home visitation."

"What happened to your mother, exactly?" she asked. "Doesn't it require a lot to put a child in foster care?" She'd thought the death of his mother had been

the reason for him entering the system. "How did she...
die?" she asked, as gently as she could.

"The time they visited, Mom was passed out on
the sofa, bottles scattered around her and the house
in shambles. One look around the house, dishes piled
in the sink, clothes all over the place, and me looking
like the thug I was turning into and I was immediately
taken from her on the spot," he answered, his voice
clipped.

Emma closed her eyes and leaned against him, trying
to lend support in the only way she could.

"It was supposed to be temporary. Turned out it was
permanent. She never came to visit while I was there.
They said she never returned the calls they sent, either.
It turns out the minute I was taken away she took off.
A few years later I was notified that she'd died."

"God, baby...baby, I'm so sorry..."

"It's okay. *I'm* okay. But it took me getting into a hell
of a lot of trouble to wise up. And that was because of
Kyle. For a long time, as far back as I could remember, I
thought I hadn't been 'man' enough to help my mother.
I hadn't been what she needed, that somehow I was
responsible for my dad leaving and for her dying."

"You were only a child. You weren't responsible—"

"I know that now. It just took me a long time to
understand it. It took an even longer time for me to
believe it."

As he spoke, his voice low, telling her how, when
Kyle brought him to Sweetwater Trail and shared his
story with him, Shane finally realized that it wasn't

his fault. How at that moment he realized his life was his own and that what he chose to do with it was up to him.

"I guess it's where I kinda laid to rest some of the old ghosts," he finished.

Emma struggled with the feelings his tale had stirred, struggled with her own ghosts, the ones that made her feel much as he had.

The feeling that she wasn't good enough.

He turned to her. She swallowed hard, seeing the pain in his eyes. "I've been alone my whole life, Emma. With the exception of Kyle…the jumpers. I'm not sure I'm looking for anything else. Anyone else. You deserve someone better than me. Someone who can—"

She placed a finger over his mouth, halting his words.

"I've been alone my whole life, too, Shane." She turned away from him, swallowing down the emotion that threatened to overwhelm her.

"I've enjoyed being with you. Making love to you. And when our time is over, well…"

He pulled her back around to face him.

"You deserve more than that, Emma. You deserve someone who can love you. Someone who can take care of you, give you what you need." His worried gaze traveled over her face, and Emma forced a smile on her mouth.

"Let's just enjoy the time we have now. I learned a long time ago that nothing is promised beyond today. I can take care of myself." While she spoke the confident words, she didn't know that she was trying to convince Shane of the truth of her words as much as herself.

He started to speak again but stopped and nodded. Standing, he reached a hand out, and Emma placed hers within his and he brought her to her feet, keeping their fingers intertwined, hands linked.

Emma stared down at his hand, feeling the warmth and the slight roughness, along with the tingling she always felt whenever he touched her. Then she looked up at him, seeing a truth reflected in his light eyes. A truth that told her that his feelings were more involved than he was willing to admit. A truth that told her he wasn't ready to let her go, despite his attempt to try.

Arms wrapped around each other, they turned and silently headed back up the trail.

Chapter 18

"Hey, you," Emma whispered softly. Filtered light and shadow shifted along the sculpted planes of his face, her mouth inches from his. "I was just dreaming about you."

"Hey, you. I was dreaming of you, too," he answered huskily, before claiming her lips with his.

The kiss was the spark that led them down the heady path of carnal bliss. He layered the kiss with sweeps of his tongue across her mouth, slowly nibbling her lips in small biting caresses.

With a tight groan, he brought both hands to the back of her head, tugged her close and slid his fingers beneath her tangled tresses. Lightly massaging her scalp, he angled her head for a better fit.

Emma opened her mouth to his when his tongue

pressed against the seam of her lips, her tongue eagerly seeking his as their kiss deepened. Bringing her hands up, she ran them over the hard wall of his chest, trailed them down until she reached his stomach, stopping when she reached the soft thatch of hair below.

When her hands found what they had been looking for, she grasped his shaft in one hand, circling as much of him as she could with her fingers, groaning when he quickly grew too thick for her hand to contain him.

She whimpered against his mouth when he broke their kiss and pulled away from her, both of them breathing heavily.

"Shane…" Her protest was cut short when he brought her hands back up and above her head, grasped within both of his.

"None of that. It'll be over before it starts. And I have plans for you." The promise was whispered coarsely against the corner of her mouth.

Liquid heat eased down her leg. "Oh yeah? What kind of plans?"

With his free hand, he trailed his fingers down her body until he reached the apex of her thighs.

"Oh, Shane…" Her breath caught when he delved a finger between her dewy lips, swirling a finger around her clitoris.

Although the light was next to nonexistent in the dark tent, his bright blue gaze gleamed with the clarity of his intent shining from within. He brought his finger to his mouth and licked it clean of her essence.

She tasted so damn good.

Shane licked a line from the tip of her chin down the line of her neck and beyond.

When he lapped a rough caress across one long, taut nipple before trailing a scorching path across the valley of her breasts, her body arched high, a long hiss escaping from her lips.

"Shane…" she whispered, the throaty moan barely audible. "Baby, please…"

He released her breast and again covered her mouth with his, drinking in her protests.

"I want to make this perfect for you."

When she placed her small hands on his face, he closed his eyes and turned into her caress. It was such a simple thing, the gesture.

Yet whenever she touched his face, framing it with her small hands, the move was so sexy and sweet at the same time that his heart constricted, the feeling almost painful in its intensity.

"You always have. Like no one else."

The raw emotion, the sincerity in her voice, shook him even more.

He'd never felt for anyone else what he did for Emma. And he hadn't a clue what to do with the newfound feelings. He had no experience in this area. Like a rookie on his first jump, he was a mass of nerves when he was around her. When she smiled up at him, her soft brown eyes filled with an emotion he was sure she was unaware they showed.

It was unfamiliar, raw and unlike anything he'd ever felt for anyone else. And it broke him down on levels he wasn't ready to examine.

Back at the site he'd tried to break free, for her sake more than for his. The thought of hurting her when the relationship inevitably ended was intolerable to him.

She deserved more, more than what he thought he had to give, because all he could give her at this time was this and nothing else.

"Mmm, you make me feel so good," she moaned breathlessly.

He slid down her body until his face was level with her breasts. Slowly he ran his fingers along her silky skin until he cupped her breasts, his thumbs brushing across their peaks, watching in lustful fascination, as each one spiked long and hard beneath his touch.

"That's what I'm trying to do," he replied, a touch of humor in his sleep-roughened voice before he lowered his mouth.

With near reverence, his tongue swiped out to bathe her nipple, rolling over the extended nub until she wiggled and whimpered beneath him, her hands tugging tightly on his hair as she pressed his face closer.

Every squirm, every shiver and moan was his reward. With no thought to his own needs, he made love to her breasts with his hands and lips.

He wanted her badly, ached to go deep, to bury himself inside her body until neither one of them knew where one started and the other began…he wanted to give her pleasure she'd never forget. Spread out in front of him, her beauty made his heart slam against his chest. He wanted to get her on all fours and penetrate her completely, spread her soft thighs, slide deep inside and lose himself within her body.

He wanted to love her until there was no thought of another, so that no man would ever be able to compare to him. The thought was a selfish one, knowing their time together was short, but he didn't give a damn. She was his. She always would be.

"You like that, baby?" he asked, his words warming her breasts as he stroked. Before she could stutter out a response, he opened his mouth wide and engulfed as much of her breast inside his mouth as possible.

Feeling a strange immediacy of the moment, he lifted his head and gazed down at her, seeing her as though for the first time. Or the last.

So beautiful. She was so incredibly beautiful. Her smell, her taste…everything about her was intoxicating to his senses, driving him wild with need.

With a growl, he grabbed her wrists again, placing her hands above her head and kissing his way down her body. Carefully, gently, as though she were a fragile piece of crystal, he separated her legs, lifting them until she was left exposed to his gaze.

He felt her body tremble beneath his touch as he feathered just the tips of his fingers across the springy curls that protected her entry. Releasing her hands, he fingered her moist lips apart, pressing a finger deep inside her body…

The rain falling against the tent became nature's soft, sensual background music accompanying the sighs and moans within.

* * *

Despite the warmth of the sleeping bag, Emma shivered violently from his hot caresses. When Shane had brushed a finger across her mound, her breath hitched as she breathlessly waited for what he'd do next. She didn't have to wait long.

When a thick finger slid inside her, a strangled cry erupted from her and her body arched away from the sleeping bag.

Her walls clenched and grabbed his finger as his lips laid claim to the nub of her femininity, stroking and kissing her until she grew dizzy, her cries of pleasure ringing out sharply in the tent as he made quiet, intense love to her.

Shane groaned against her folds. One long swipe of his tongue deep inside her, and her body detonated. Emma slapped her palms down, her body shaking so hard she could barely move, straining against the hold he had on her.

"Shannnnnne…" she wailed, her head on the sleeping bag, her heartbeat stuttering against her chest.

He didn't release her until the last of her cries had died down to whimpering moans and panting breaths, hard tremors shaking her legs.

Strung out, her body a liquid mass, Emma was afraid to move. The slightest movement caused tendrils of sensation to curl throughout her body, one big mass of oversensitive nerves.

But he wasn't done with her. The look in his eyes told her he had even more decadent plans in mind. She was lightheaded, dizzy, his touch intoxicating.

He turned, fumbling in the semidark tent in search of protection, and was back seconds later, covering her body with his.

He lifted her up, wrapping her legs around his waist slowly and driving himself deep inside her in one long plunge.

On and on he drove into her, his thrusts becoming wilder with every stroke until Emma screamed, passion exploding behind her tightly clenched eyelids. He reared back, digging his fingers into the skin of her legs, and delivered two more strokes before throwing his head back as the fall of rain became harder, the sound of wind and rain deafening.

"I love you, Emma. I love you!"

At that moment, she came, her cries of release blended with his stunning exclamation…both lost in the sound of the rain.

Their lovemaking had alternated between fast and raw, when he'd slipped between her legs and had her so hot and ready she climaxed within minutes, and long and sweet, with their undulating bodies and swaying hips in perfect rhythm, their lovemaking drawn out, deliberate and intense.

Whatever method, it hadn't mattered; the result had been the same. Each and every time it had been mind-blowing, leaving them both breathless, satiated…and somehow still wanting more.

At one point she'd thought she'd heard him say he loved her. She adjusted her body, glancing down at him, but he'd been asleep, his face nestled in the hollow of her throat.

In sleep, the lines that bracketed his mouth had appeared softer, making him look younger, vulnerable. Entranced, she'd continued her silent perusal of him, realizing it was the first time she'd seen him, even after the many times they'd made love, so…at ease. Even in sleep he always seemed aware, as though he never fully relaxed.

His eyes had opened and a ghost of a smile flirted around the corners of his mouth as he caught her perusal of him. Without a word, he'd flipped her beneath them, and rained kisses across her face.

Yet the peaceful, relaxed image of him had remained in her mind as they made love. She'd tucked it, as well as the other images of him she'd began to mentally store away, for a time to revisit later, when her assignment was over.

A time when she'd once again be alone.

She sighed, not wanting to think of when that time would come, realizing she had only a few weeks left at the station before they would have to say goodbye. Troubled, she tried to fall asleep, her body curling into his.

Chapter 19

Emma woke and turned toward Shane, expecting to feel him next to her, their limbs intertwined around each other, as she had many times throughout the night. Instead, she encountered empty space beneath the double-down sleeping bag when she reached for him.

She opened her eyes and rose up slowly, her foggy mind gradually piecing together the events from the day before. Crawling from beneath the covers, she fumbled around until she found Shane's shirt and drew it over her head and located her discarded panties from the night before and pulled them on.

She walked outside the tent, the sun's early morning rays filtering through the thicket of trees greeting her.

She stopped and inhaled deeply, the morning air

carrying a sachet of smells—wildflowers, earth and nature.

Her gaze searched out and found Shane. Standing not far away, near his truck with his bare back toward her, wearing nothing but low-slung jeans. In his hand was a mug of what she assumed was coffee, his thumb absently tracing around the rim.

He turned and placed the coffee cup on the hood of his car, and she caught a glimpse of his face. From that distance, she could see the way his brow was furrowed, a contemplative look on his face.

When he caught sight of her, he paused in the act, turned and fully faced her, his expression lightening. A slow smile replaced the frown. He held out his hand, inviting her to join him, pulling the mug from the hood of the truck. Putting the look she'd seen and the possible cause from her mind, Emma made her way over to him.

Shane's eyes flew open when he felt Emma's fidgeting body move against his.

In her sleep she tossed, restlessly moving her body, a deep frown on her face, mumbling incoherent words in an oddly childlike voice.

He bent his head toward her, listening carefully, finally making out her words.

"Mommy, Daddy, please don't go. Please don't leave me again. I wanna go with you guys this time," she begged. "I promise I won't be in the way!" She began crying seconds later.

As he listened to her murmuring, he realized she

was locked inside her dream world, repeating her crying pleas to her parents, tugging on his heart until it ached.

There was a pause. As she slept, her face took on a look similar to that of a frightened child, her full bottom lip poking out, trembling. Tears fell down her cheeks, her lips quivering as she softly cried.

"Sssh, it's okay, baby. I'm not going anywhere." Shane gathered her body close to his, murmuring soft, reassuring words until she quieted down.

He held her that way until her soft snores alerted him that she was no longer trapped inside the dream. His soothing words and gentle touch finally relaxed her body, no longer tossing in agitation, a calm finally settling over her.

He stared at her face for a long time, her body curled trustingly around his, hand rested on his chest. He lifted it and opened her palm, giving a soft kiss to the center before laying it back on his chest.

"I love you, Emma."

The words he said came back and slapped him in the face.

He'd said more things than he wanted to remember in the heat of the moment when making love to a woman. But one thing he'd never said were those three words.

He turned from her, running his hands through his hair, staring into the near darkness, the only illumination coming from the small lantern he'd placed outside their tent to ward off any curious nocturnal creatures.

Assured she was sleeping peacefully, Shane eased

his body away from Emma's and stood. Throwing on the jeans from the previous day, he left the tent, his thoughts filled with Emma and the tantalizing question running through his mind that they could be together.

As he looked at her now, watching her from the entry of their tent, that curious ache blossomed in his heart again. He held his hand out, and she moved toward him.

Without a word, he pulled her into his arms and held her tightly.

It was time to head back home. Back to reality.

Chapter 20

"Yeah, that's what your mouth says!" Emma shot back, lining up her stick to the cue ball, leaning down over the pool table. "Let's see you put your money where your mouth is, son!"

"Son? Okay, little girl, show me what you got," Shane replied, smirking.

Emma pulled back and made the shot. The hard crack of the cue ball hitting the eight ball, sending it spinning, banking off the back rail and neatly sliding into the corner pocket, split the air. Emma spun around, raising a brow, a cocky grin on her face.

"Did that show you?" She smirked, putting out her hand. "Okay, now pay up!"

Before she realized his intent, he grabbed her

around her waist, hauling her against his body, her toes dangling off the floor.

She squealed, slapping her hand against his chest. "Hey, no fair! You pay with money, not with kisses. Kisses won't pay the rent," she quipped.

He wrapped both arms around her snugly as his gaze roamed over her face.

"What? Do I have something on my face?" she asked, self-consciously swiping her fingers over her mouth.

After Shane had suggested they not return to the station, and instead spend another two days together at his place, they'd spent the entire first day and long into the night just making love to each other.

They hadn't even gotten out of the bed, had simply enjoyed the pleasure of being with one another, uninterrupted, just the two of them. The only time they'd been out had been to eat, and even then they'd taken the food to the bed and afterward made love in the crumbs.

The last four days had been the best she'd had in a long time. The trip to Sweetwater, where she and Shane had spent the time relaxing, making love and learning about each other, to now, where they played…and made love.

For the first time in her life, Emma felt completely at ease.

It was Tuesday evening, their last night away together. Both had agreed they needed to actually get out of bed. Shane had threatened that he was not a man restrained to the confines of the bed when loving his woman.

Emma had blushed, partly because of the threat, partly because of his casual reference that she was his.

Emma forced herself to stop over-thinking it. Forced herself to stop wondering if and when she'd wake up from the dream, feeling as though the last few weeks had been like a fairy tale.

Take life as it comes. That had been her motto for so long, the words automatically came to her mind. Accept it as it comes, and don't expect too much. It was a surefire way of avoiding pain and heartache.

"No. You're beautiful," he said, responding to her question.

"Shane…" The word was whispered, her eyes fluttering shut to block out the expression on his face. An expression she refused to analyze and try and figure out. Refused to dare hope that he could possibly share her feelings, feelings she'd just discovered she had for him.

She clenched her eyes tightly for a moment longer, fighting against the unexpected sting she felt burning at the back of them.

She had it bad for him. There was no fooling herself otherwise. When she felt his hands tighten on her waist, her eyes flew open, seeking his.

He lifted her until her feet left the floor, suspended with nothing but his strong arms around her holding her upright. He slowly lowered his head and covered her mouth with his.

Emma sighed into his kiss. She wrapped her arms around his neck, completely giving over to his caress. One of his hands remained around her waist, easily holding her firmly against his side, while the other tunneled beneath her hair at the nape of her neck.

"Mmm...I love kissing you." The coarse whisper feathered against her mouth. He pulled away and allowed her body to slide against his until her feet touched the floor.

God, what he did to her. The way he made her feel with just one kiss. One touch. One look... Emma reached a hand toward his mouth, up, tracing her finger over the bottom curve of his sensual lips, her finger shaky. He drew the digit deeply into his mouth, his bright eyes on hers, swirling the pad of her finger around his tongue and suckling the flesh.

Heat radiated from his body, the flare of desire burning bright in his eyes as he licked and suckled her finger.

"Let's get out of here," he finally said, his voice low, husky with need.

She slowly became aware of her surroundings as he lowered her. Before she could be anything more than mildly embarrassed at their shameless display, he laid claim to her mouth again. A shrill ring brought her back to reality.

He broke their kiss, swearing lightly, and blindly reached down to snatch his cell phone from his pocket.

"Yes," he bit out, his voice impatient, his heated gaze still on Emma. Emma's fingers brushed against the frown, and immediately he smiled.

When the smile slipped from his face, Emma gave him a questioning look.

As he listened, Emma felt his hold tightening on her, yet he continued to hold her.

"I'll be there in ten minutes."

He ended the conversation, placing his cell back on his belt clip.

"What's wrong?"

"There's a situation brewing near the Idaho-Montana border. Everything is under control for now, but we'd better head back just in case," he said, smiling briefly as he turned with her and strode briskly out of the bar.

"Do they need reinforcements?" she asked as they reached his truck.

"Not yet. Everything looks under control. They *are* in need of more supplies. Some of the guys were scheduled for a practice jump, so on the way we'll parachute down some supplies."

"We?" she asked, her excitement growing, thinking he was including her.

"*We* as in me and a few others. You will be safely tucked away at the station," he replied firmly, starting the engine and peeling out of the parking lot.

"Tucked away? No, you didn't! Give me a break, Shane! Let me come! I could get some great pictures—"

"Emma, I already told you, no live-fire missions! This is serious work. You could get hu—"

"Shane, I'm a big girl! I can handle myself!" She interrupted him this time. Even as the words left her mouth, he was already shaking his head no.

"Absolutely not. When we get back to the station you can go to the ground crew area. I'm sure there will be more than enough things going on for you to get plenty of information for your article."

"Shane. Come *on.* An opportunity like this doesn't come around often. I'm only here for a short time more. This is perfect!"

He turned to her. "No, Emma. I'm sorry, but it's just too dangerous. Fires can, and *do,* move. Anything can pop off once we're airborne. I don't want to take the chance with you on board."

"I can handle myself," she insisted. "Besides, this might be my only chance to catch a live shot from the air. I can get the kind of shots that could make or break this article. Make it go national. Please, Shane," she all but begged, but yet again he was shaking his head no before she could even finish her sentence.

"Emma, I don't have time for this. Not now. Please."

She expelled a deep breath, crossing her arms over her chest, clenching her jaw tight. Finally she nodded her head. "Fine."

A look of relief eased over his face before he sped along the street, heading back toward base.

The station was teeming with action when Emma and Shane arrived. As soon as they entered, Roebuck called out to Shane and the two of them quickly made their way to the control room where he briefed them on the latest developments.

"The situation is unchanged—the fire is being contained," Roebuck said as soon as they joined him at the computer monitor. He pointed to an area on the map where the fire was currently raging. "They have enough men. Jumpers from Montana have already lent additional manpower, so everything is under control."

"Thank God."

"The only thing our men are doing is setting up a paracargo drop, lending more supplies. The men assigned were headed up to a nearby area anyway, to do a practice jump."

"Plan still the same?" Shane asked.

"Yes. As soon as the cargo is parachuted down, they'll go to the area for their jump." He turned to Emma, including her. "I thought this might be a great opportunity for Emma to get some live shots. Maybe you could take her up with you."

"No way! Emma isn't going anywhere near a live mission!" Shane stated firmly.

Emma turned to Shane, a pleading look on her face, and he was already shaking his head no.

"Oh, come on, Shane!"

"No, it's out of the question. Anything can happen. You'd have to wear a chute…"

"I've taken the course. I've watched the film, remember?"

"You haven't jumped, though, Emma."

"I've jumped before, Shane! You know that. Not here, not into a fire, but I know how to use a parachute!" When he looked as though he was going to argue more, she interrupted him, "Besides, I won't have to jump! I'm just going along for the ride, to get the pictures. And you'll be there with me. Nothing is going to happen, Shane."

Her shoulders slumped when she saw the flat line of his mouth not budge. He gave her a quick frown and turned to go. When he reached the door he paused before turning back to face her.

A resigned look crossed his face, and after a slight hesitation he said, "Come with me. We have to get you outfitted if you're going to fly with us."

Emma let out a whoop and ran toward him, grabbing him around the neck and giving him a big hug. "Thank you, Shane! I promise I'll follow your instructions! Let me grab my camera and I'll meet you and the crew in the cargo area!"

Before he could change his mind, she sprinted out the door and ran to his truck to retrieve her camera before making her way back to the hangar to join him and the other crew, now forming, preparing to go.

"This way, Emma," Shane said as soon as she joined them. She quickly followed him as he led her to the "suit-up racks" in the ready room, where he grabbed suits for the both of them.

Emma quickly donned the gear, thankful for the boring training films he'd made her suffer through that demonstrated the quick and efficient way to put on gear.

When she finished dressing, just seconds after Shane, she glanced over at him. She walked closer to him, placing a finger over his ever-present frown, and smoothed a finger over the deep lines etched into his forehead.

"I'll follow your instructions, Shane. I promise. You can trust me."

He captured her finger, giving it a soft kiss before nodding his head. "You know I can't say no to you."

She grinned up at him. "No, I didn't know that. But it's good info to know," she quipped.

"Let's go, woman!" he growled, and Emma hid her smile.

Chapter 21

An air of excitement and expectation prevailed inside the plane.

Besides Emma and Shane, there were the four jumpers who were going out for their practice shoot, a spotter and the pilot. The remainder of the "crew" consisted of boxes of supplies that were to be parachuted down to the jumpers on the mission in Montana.

"We're headed over the Grand Tetons, and from there we'll parachute the cargo down just on the other side of the mountain."

With her face pressed to the window, Emma saw the mountains come into view and gasped when she saw a shadow of dark smoke darken the skies.

"We're coming close to the fire. It's contained so

far," Shane said in answer to her unspoken question, his voice grim.

The cargo was to be sent down to the men below, before the jumpers would precede to their jump site. Both the pilot and Shane were in constant contact with the ground crew being updated on the fire.

"What if—"

"Shane, I think you'd better come up here. The situation has changed," the pilot called out loudly over the loud engine, interrupting Emma.

"Hold that thought, baby," Shane said, swiftly making his way over to the pilot. Hunching down low, he and the pilot spoke in tones too low for Emma to hear, yet she noticed immediately the change that came over Shane.

"Change in plans," he said grimly, walking back toward Emma and the four jumpers, who all immediately stood, gathering around Shane.

"The fire has shifted, growing in a new direction. The son of a bitch barreled right past the containment field. It's growing too fast and it's getting out of control. There aren't enough jumpers to handle it. They're calling in backup. We're headed that way and we're the closest ones. Thank God we're minutes away."

The men nodded their heads, quickly preparing for the jump. Although the news was grim, it wasn't completely unexpected.

Shane turned to Emma.

"You're fine. There's no danger to you, but still…"

"Shane, handle your business, baby. I know how to

stay safe. Nothing will happen. You have enough to worry about other than me right now."

"*You* stay safe."

"I will," she promised.

Despite the tension of the moment, he yanked the glove from his hand, ran a finger down her face and leaned down to give her a soft kiss.

He turned back to the men, his voice losing the intimacy, becoming brisk as he briefed them on the change in the situation.

Neither he nor Emma noticed—or cared—the way the others turned away, smiles on their faces despite the tension, after the small intimacy. Their senior squad leader was known for his brisk manner, yet whenever he was around Emma he softened noticeably.

Shane's worried glance fell on Emma, her camera on her lap, a contemplative look on her face.

She must have felt his gaze on hers. Turning in his direction, she offered him a reassuring smile, yet the smile appeared strained, the worry in her soft brown eyes easy to see.

For the first time in his career as a jumper, the anxiety he felt churning in his gut had nothing to do with the mission ahead, or the lives in jeopardy. Instead his anxiety had to do with the small woman who had, in one short month, come into his life and turned it upside down.

He forced a reassuring smile before he turned away to face the others.

"We're nearing the drop site," Jones, the spotter,

called out over the near-deafening roar of wind and engine, listening to the direction from the pilot.

Again Shane's gaze flew over to Emma. No longer looking in his direction, she'd returned her attention to her camera, gazing out the window. He wanted— needed—to go over to her one last time to reassure her. But all of his attention needed to be on the mission ahead.

He fingered the cross around his neck in the same way he did each time before he jumped. Pausing before tucking it inside his jumpsuit, he glanced down at it.

Kyle had given him it to him. It had been passed down from his grandfather to his father, and then to Kyle, once he joined the jumpers. Kyle had given it to him the day he graduated from his rookie class. He'd never jumped a fire without it. Until now.

Briskly, he walked back toward Emma, lifted the necklace from around his neck and placed it around hers. Without a word he turned around and made his way to the back.

The doors opened to the thunderous roar of wind, immediately revealing a billowing column of smoke rising high. When the spotter pulled his head back inside the plane, he yelled over the roar of wind, "Take us down to three thousand."

It was time. The jumpers pulled on their helmets and flipped the wire-mesh mask over their faces before tugging on gloves. All of them, including Shane, were running on pumped-up adrenaline, like horses at the starting line. They were primed and ready for the start- ing gun and the race to begin.

After the spotter gave the go sign, Shane led the way. At the door he paused, glancing over his shoulder once more at Emma before dropping into a sitting position, legs dangling out of the plane.

When he felt the slap on the back from the spotter, he grabbed his toggles and peered below.

His gaze scanned the column of smoke that cast an ominous shadow over the land below as he leaped from the plane, his body pitching sideways against the heavy wind, beginning the familiar mental countdown: "Jump-thousand, look thousand…"

Chapter 22

Emma stood as near as possible to the jump door, capturing each man's jump on film, until the last one left.

Although her stomach was in knots with worry over the danger the men—Shane—were literally jumping into, she continued to take picture after picture, long after the last jumper was too far from the plane to capture his image through the smoke and fire obscuring her vision.

The beauty of the images was indescribable, haunting. She hoped she'd captured the near otherworldly quality on film. For the first time in her career as a photojournalist, she was not only in awe, but felt strangely inadequate, fearing that her skills wouldn't—couldn't—do them justice.

She'd gotten to know the jumpers on a personal level. Their humor, who they were as individuals, why each one had joined the smoke jumpers…each man had a different tale, a different story to what brought him to this point in his life.

"Did you get what you needed, Emma?" There was a subdued quality to the spotter's voice, and she turned to face him, nodding her head.

"Yeah, I think I did."

With a soft clap on the back, he turned and signaled the pilot to close the doors, and Emma moved back to take her seat. She stared out the window, sightless, trying to muscle her mind away from thinking about the danger Shane was facing and to concentrate on the article she still needed to write.

Over the last month, she'd captured more than enough images to sift through later and decide which ones would make the cut, but she knew the lasting image in her mind of Shane placing his beloved cross around her neck before jumping from the plane was the one that would stick in her mind forever.

She fingered the necklace.

Sighing, she grabbed her backpack, glad she'd retrieved it from Shane's truck before leaving, and withdrew her voice recorder. Hovering in the recesses of her mind was the angle she needed, the one that she saw with an instant's clarity was the direction to take for her article.

"Jones, I need you up here!"

Urgency rang sharply in the pilot's voice as he called the spotter, cutting into her thoughts. Emma rose from her seat as the spotter strode swiftly past her. As she rose, a violent turbulence hit. The plane dipped, the impact shoving her violently to the side, the side of her head hitting the corner of the seat in front of her, her backpack spilling to the floor.

Righting herself, she took a shaky breath as the plane dipped once more before leveling off and swiped her hands over her jumpsuit. Carefully Emma stood, her hands braced on the top of the seat in front of her.

Grabbing the overhead cable, she carefully made her way to the front, where the pilot and spotter were in frantic conversation.

"It's collapsing! If we don't get word to them——"

"What? What's going on?" Emma broke in.

The spotter turned to her. "The situation has turned from sugar to salt, real quick. A smoke column is starting to collapse."

"And what does that mean?" Emma cut in, her head swiveling from one man to the other as they both spoke, simultaneously, fear making her almost want to gag. She swallowed it down, and with her heart jackhammering in her chest, listened as both men began to explain, relieved they didn't try and sugarcoat the situation or exclude her from what was happening.

"Weather can contribute to the spread of forest fires—by way of drought, lightning, wind. They create their own weather, and the result is catastrophic, creating pyro-cumulous clouds."

She frowned, looking from one man to the other. "Again…what does that mean?"

The spotter—Jones—turned to face Emma. "What

it means is this— Imagine a monster of flames that rises up to spit out thunder and lightning. This fire has become large and powerful enough that it's now creating its own weather system. It's called a blow-up. The smoke column has grown out of control. The top is thirty thousand feet, and it's growing…the fire is feeding it."

Shivers danced along Emma's spine at the deadly picture Jones described.

"And it's about to collapse."

"We need to let the jumpers know what's happening, now. If we don't…"

Without warning, the plane began to quake. Bouncing, it tipped crazily to the side, and Emma screamed even as the violent rocking slammed her into the seat. Had she not quickly wrapped her arms around the seat in front of her, her head would have slammed into the small window.

With a hiss of pain, she gingerly touched her forehead, wincing. Her fingers came away stained, sticky with her own blood.

"Are you okay?" The pilot shouted the words over his shoulder, barely glancing at her, his attention solely on battling the wind hammering into the plane.

Emma rose, swallowed down the instant nausea and raced over to Jones when she spotted him lying on the floor, eyes closed.

She kneeled down beside him, grabbed him by the shoulders and shook him, yelling his name, but he didn't respond.

"Oh, God!" Emma cried out when his eyes remained closed. "He's not responding...he's unconscious!"

"The radio's dead." Both Emma and the pilot spoke at the same time.

They met each other's gaze, and the same fear and panic that Emma was feeling was reflected in the pilot's eyes.

Emma swallowed, her throat gone completely dry. "What do we do now?"

With his face set in grim lines, he answered, "Do you think you can parachute down and tell them?"

Chapter 23

Shane had been the first man to hit the ground.

Within moments of landing, he was casting off his chute, along with the rest of the jumpers hot on his heels, running at full speed toward the site.

Quickly joining the Idaho team of jumpers, he and his men were fully engaged in fighting the fire, doing their best to contain it before it grew out of control.

"Who the hell is that?"

One of the jumpers near him yelled and Shane looked up, his eyes narrowing as he squinted behind his protective mask.

"No way on earth is that Emma!" he exploded, his heart pounding in his chest. Under the parachute, she drew down close enough so that he could see her waving her arms and pointing toward the west.

"What the hell is she pointing at, and what the hell is she doing jumping, damn it!"

He frowned, turning toward the direction she was waving. Dread pooled in his gut when he realized what was happening.

In the distance, the small smoke column had increased, growing to unbearable proportions; it wouldn't be long before it would collapse.

His gaze shifted back to Emma.

Icy cold fingers of dread gripped his pounding heart, and fear slamming into him in nauseating waves. A shift in wind was slowly moving her descending figure away from him.

She was heading directly into the blazing column.

With no thought, Shane took off at a full run toward Emma, several jumpers on his heels. He yelled over his shoulder, "I'll take care of her. Just keep working the fire, damn it!"

"Shane, no way in hell can you get to her. The wind is taking her too far away!" one of the jumpers yelled from behind him, but Shane ignored the man and kept running toward Emma.

Adrenaline coursed a fiery path in his veins. Shane picked up speed and threw his pack off his back to lighten his body. As he continued to run toward her, the column that had been building collapsed, and immediately downdrafts began to blow down, swiftly spreading a vicious lick of fire separating her from him.

Forced to retreat, Shane cursed, quickly backpedaling

away from the rapidly growing fire before making a headlong dive behind a large rock slide.

When the wind bowed, moving Emma toward the smoke column, she swiftly called to memory every training video on emergency landing Shane had forced her to watch. Fighting for her life, she managed to get the chute in control, steering it away from the direction it was heading.

Once she landed, she did a quick assessment of the situation, realizing the fire was rapidly burning a path toward her.

She sent a prayer heavenward before running like hell up the slope of the mountain. Her lungs began to burn with her Herculean effort to outrace the fire. After realizing there was no way she could, she stopped and shoved away her useless tears, knowing that time was not her friend. Any moment, the flames would catch up with her.

Scanning the area, she nearly fainted in relief when she spotted an old mine shaft not far ahead, near the edge of the mountainside. Remembering the story of Ranger Pulaski—another old video Shane had forced her to watch—and how the firefighter had used a mine shaft to save his and several others' lives, she raced toward it.

Using up every last bit of strength and adrenaline, she managed to make it to the shaft and run inside, saving herself from the immediate danger.

She quickly entered the smoky shaft, and just as the ranger and his crew did, she immediately lay facedown on the ground, hoping—praying—that the shaft would provide her with protection.

She didn't know how long she lay there. Minutes… hours, it was all a blur. She drifted off to sleep, her mind and body too tired to remain awake, the adrenaline dissipated, feeling nothing but utter exhaustion.

Just as swiftly as she had fallen asleep, her eyes opened and her body jerked her into a sitting position, and for a moment panic seized her, squeezing the air from her lungs.

Hyperventilating behind the protective mask, her fingers clawed at the mesh-wire opening in an attempt to get air, before she stopped, forcing her panic at bay.

She was safe. She peered around, squinting behind the helmet.

Although not completely clear, the air appeared to be smoke free. Her chest heaving, she brought the brewing panic attack firmly under control and carefully removed the helmet, allowing it fall to the gravel-covered ground beside her.

She took deep, calming breaths of air through her nose, slowly exhaling it out of her opened mouth. It was clear. Licking her dry lips, she closed her eyes briefly before glancing around the dark, abandoned mine shaft.

Slowly, tears began to trickle down her face.

Her teeth started to chatter and her body shook violently as the tears gained momentum. She drew her knees to her chest, wrapping her arms around her bent legs and giving in to the emotional release.

She was safe.

* * *

"Emma!"

Emma was jolted out of her light sleep upon hearing the hoarse cry.

Her head jerked toward the entry of the mine shaft. Standing there was Shane. With a cry, she rose, her knees buckling. She'd only taken a few stumbling steps when he caught her, lifted her into his arms and held her tightly in his grasp.

"Oh God, oh God, oh God…baby, you're okay…oh God, you're okay!"

Emma trembled in his grasp, hearing the terror mingled with relief in his voice, her cries that had finally come to a halt returning, clogging her throat.

She wrapped her arms around him just as tightly as he held her, his hold on her nearly painful it was so tight.

After a few long moments, he finally pulled her away from him. He hastily yanked off his gloves and, tilting her face up to his, stared down at her. It was then that Emma saw the tears that streaked his soot-covered face, the ravaged look in his bright blue eyes.

"Damn you, Emma! You could have gotten someone killed!" The arms that held her at arm's length shook. With a groan, he grabbed her and pulled her back against his body.

When he finally pulled away, his angry gaze ran over her, and she stood still. His rage was a tangible thing—he was angrier than she'd ever seen him. Helplessly, she stared up at him, unable to move.

"Shane…I…I was scared for you! Jones was knocked

out in the turbulence. The column was collapsing, the radio died…" Her sputtering words ended on a small cry when his hands tightened on her arms. Emma squirmed away from his punishing hold, her breasts pressed flush against his hard unyielding chest, the faint smell of smoke clinging to his big body.

"You could have gotten yourself killed." He bit the words out, his fingers digging into her arms.

She reached a hesitant hand out as though to touch him, and he grabbed her wrist before it made contact with his face.

"Shane…" The plea came out as little more than a whisper.

Both of their breathing was harsh, his face set, his jaw clenched tightly. The small tic in the corner of his sensual mouth and the emotion swirling in his bright blue gaze were the only indication of his feelings.

She licked her bottom lip. When he followed the action with his gaze, the tic in the corner of his mouth grew even more pronounced, and every instinct in her told her to run. Run like hell and put as much distance between him and her as humanly possible.

Snatching her wrist away from his punishing grasp, she spun away. She'd gotten no farther than a few steps before he was on her. Whipping her body around, he shook her until her teeth rattled.

"Shane!" she cried out. Not from any pain, but out of trepidation from the look in his eyes as he glared down at her.

Grabbing her by the waist, he lifted her, cradling her in his arms, before walking deeper into the narrow shaft in long, swift strides and lowering her on the ground.

"I need you, Emma," he said, kissing her, stroking a shaky hand down the line of her throat.

Emma ran a desirous glance over him, searching out his eyes, her pulse quickening, stuttering, hammering against her chest.

He opened his big hand, flattening it against the hollow of her throat in both a possessive and dominant move.

"Oh God, baby…I'm sorry—" Her words were again interrupted by his mouth and the hot glide of his tongue against hers.

Emma moaned into his kiss, raising her body when his hands impatiently tugged at her suit, pulling it completely from her body, helping him to rid her of her clothing.

Within seconds she lay beneath him, wearing nothing but his T-shirt, the same one she'd put on hours before when they were at his home, and a pair of panties. Without a word he lifted her onto her knees and placed her in front of his body, grasping her waist and bringing her tight against his shaft.

She heard the hiss of his zipper and glanced over her shoulder. She swallowed thickly, her throat gone dry as she saw the passion-driven way he removed his own clothes, just enough to free himself. When he sprang free, thick and hard from the confines of his suit, she shut her eyes, excitement replacing her anxiety.

He lightly grasped her hair, fisting the tangled

threads around his hand and angling her head back so that they were looking into each other's eyes.

Her heart skipped a beat upon a glance at his tightly drawn features, somehow transformed by the whole ordeal into something hotter and sexier than she could have ever imagined.

When he leaned forward and placed a punishing kiss on her mouth, she whimpered, her eyes fluttering closed. Emma gasped when he bit down on her full bottom lip before releasing her hair. He placed his hand on the base of her neck, keeping her facing forward.

When she felt the knob of his shaft at her entry, she moaned, bucking her body back, welcoming him into her depths.

"Shane!" she screamed out in pleasure when he pushed himself fully inside.

"You could have gotten yourself killed..."

Emma pushed back against him, needing him as much as he needed her, the musky scent of sex and lust taking over her senses, her head dizzy with the dual assault of Shane and need hammering at her body.

He pushed into her, rocking back and forth, gliding in and out of her in short, tight, controlled thrusts while his fingers dug deep into the fleshy skin of her hips.

He lifted one of her legs, angled himself and went deeper. Emma screamed at the hot invasion, her body going up in flames as he pressed deeper inside her than ever before.

"Yes, yes yes..." she cried out, mindless in her need, her desire...her love for this man.

She drew in a strangled breath; the realization that

she was completely in love with him ricocheted into her at the same time that her body exploded.

Shutting her eyes tight, stars danced like a million fireflies behind her closed lids as she climaxed, her walls clamping down tight, milking him as she cried out her release.

Yet even as she came, he continued to rock into her. He lifted her higher, thrusting into her at a new angle. Her body pitched forward. Despite the suit he'd spread as protection, she felt the sharp edges of the rocks beneath her knees. Yet, none of that mattered as his hot strokes became more demanding. When her body reached the pinnacle again, she screamed until she grew hoarse, as another orgasm ripped through her.

She threw back her head, bucking her body against his, her eyes clenched tight. As she reached her release, she heard his harsh groans as though from a distance, his answering roar bounding off the stony walls.

Her body completely drained from the force of her climax, she would have pitched forward and fallen on her face, her limbs were so shaky, had he not maintained his hold on her.

Her head hung low, her body rocking from the strength of his continued thrusts before she heard his low, deep growl and the sweet feel of his release flood her body.

Her thighs quivered, her arms shook, her entire body was blissfully numb as he pulled out of her, before he released her, allowing her body to crumble to the ground.

Emma lay on her stomach, his hard, hot body pressing into her, thoroughly satiated. For a long moment, she lay with his chest blanketing her back, his warm breath fanning the hairs at the nape of her neck.

When he pulled away, she shivered, their combined sweat instantly cooling against her naked skin. Too weak to move, she simply lay there until she heard him speak.

"I want you gone."

"What?" She gasped, swiftly turning to see him pulling his suit back over his body in jerky movements. "What are you talking about?" Her brow furrowed as she watched him, just as quick to put his clothing on as he had been to remove it before.

When he wouldn't look at her, she simply got up and began to dress, feeling a cry of denial lodged deep in her throat.

She ground her teeth, refusing to allow it to release, even as tears burned the back of her eyes.

"You should have enough *material* to finish your article, Emma."

Emma winced at the cutting words.

"But whether you do or don't, I don't really give a damn. I want you gone by the week's end."

"Shane…I did it for you! For the men!"

When he spun around, pinning her with a hard gaze, Emma drew back, her eyes widening.

"I didn't think—"

"That's just it. You didn't think, damn it!" He shook his head and barked out a humorless laugh.

"You didn't think of anyone but yourself and your damn article," he replied, his words cutting into her like a blade—swift, harsh, deadly. "You're nothing more than a self-centered opportunist."

"I wasn't thinking of myself or the article. Listen to me, Shane, please!"

Without further reply, he spun around, his long-legged strides taking him across the cave in seconds. At the entry to the mine, he hesitated. He turned his head, barely looking over his shoulder, making no eye contact with her.

"The fire is under control. The men are cleaning up. You're safe here. Someone will be around to lead you back as soon as possible. "

"Can't I go with—"

"It won't be long," he cut in. "I won't be at the station when you return. Please be gone before I come back to base."

Again, tears ran down Emma's cheeks, this time they had nothing to do with her brush with death and everything to do with the man who thought so little of her that he believed she'd endanger the lives of others to further her career.

Emma allowed the tears free rein to fall as she watched him go.

Chapter 24

Shane scowled down at the photo in his hand, his mood dark.

The picture had been taken by one of the others when Emma, carrying the forty-pound sack, crossed the finish line during one of the training exercises.

He ran a thumb back and forth over the image. Strands of hair had escaped the ponytail at the back of her head, but despite her exhaustion, a tired, pleased smile graced her full lips as she looked up into the camera.

"Damn," he murmured.

Although she'd only been at the station a month, her absence was noticeable when he returned three days later to learn she was no longer there.

He'd caught the sidelong glances from some of the

others, questions in their eyes he had no intention on answering.

Questions he had no answers to himself.

Being back at the station had served to remind him that he'd had a slice of heaven for few short weeks with Emma. And more importantly, that he no longer had that.

"Please be gone before I come back to base."

The last words he said to her rang in his mind.

"Just like you wanted, right?" he asked aloud to the empty room.

"What did you do to her?" another voice replied.

Shane paused, stiffening, his fingers clutching the picture in one hand, the other holding a T-shirt he'd been about to place in his duffel bag. Slowly, he placed the photo in his bag along with the shirt and zipped the bag shut, keeping his back to his commander.

In the current state he was in, he was liable to say something to Roebuck he was sure to regret, so he decided to talk around the issue.

"I'm assuming you mean Emma?" he finally replied, trying damn hard to keep his tone moderate.

"Hell yeah, I mean Emma. You leave her in that goddamn mine shaft—"

"She was perfectly okay. A flight crew was approaching. They brought her down before I even made it down the hill," Shane shot back. Yet, even as he said it, he felt a moment of shame for leaving her there, for refusing to allow her to return with him. But at the time, he'd been so furious with her that all rational thought had flown out the window, anger and fear driving his actions.

"That's not the point!"

"What exactly is the point? Was the point that she pulled a crazy stunt like that where she could have gotten herself killed? Or that she endangered the lives of others trying to rescue her from the ridiculous, self-serving act in question?"

He spun around angrily to face Roebuck. "Color me confused, because I sure as hell don't know, sir. What exactly *is* the point?"

The two men stared each other down, neither one giving an inch, until finally Roebuck sighed, shook his head and walked farther into the room.

"No, the point is that she risked her own life to try and warn us that the column was about to collapse when no one else could have. She quite possibly saved the lives of a few civilians and a hell of a lot of manpower by risking her life and making the jump."

"What? I, I didn't know that." Shane stumbled back, the impact from Roebuck's admission stunning him into silence.

Roebuck fully explained what Emma had done and the reasons why. The more he talked, the lower Shane felt, realization at the magnitude of her gesture hitting him, hard. He felt lower than he ever had, anger at his own self-righteousness making him nauseous, thinking of how badly he'd hurt her.

After he'd made it back, the worst of the fire had been contained and it was at the cleanup stage. He hadn't stuck around, had simply wanted to get away from the site before he went back up and grabbed Emma again to demand she tell him what had possessed her to commit the foolhardy act.

His shoulders slumped as he sank down on his bunk. He had completely screwed everything up. She probably hated him, and she had every right to.

When he'd seen her parachuting down, every imaginable terror had entered his mind, everything from her getting caught in a tree, to her landing in the middle of the fire, and he'd felt…helpless.

Again.

"Oh God, what have I done?"

He felt the dip in the mattress when Roebuck joined him and raised his eyes to meet his commander's dark ones, filled with empathy.

"Look, I don't want to interfere with this, but—"

"No, please, go ahead. It seems like I've made a complete mess of things on my own."

"I know that a lot of your feelings about women being smoke jumpers—hell, women in general—have a lot to do with what happened to you growing up and what happened to Kyle." When Shane remained quiet, not asking how Roebuck knew of his background, he continued.

"I've watched you grow, become the man in front of me. I'll admit I wasn't exactly your champion, didn't know what the hell Kyle was thinking when he brought you to the station. But he saw something in you, something a lot of other people didn't see. Something that told him you had a future. That you weren't just another statistic waiting to happen."

Shane's hand, resting on the top of his thigh, clenched the minute Roebuck mentioned Kyle.

"But he proved me wrong. He proved a lot of us wrong. And when Kyle died, you were angry, hurt and you blamed someone you shouldn't have."

Shane didn't want to talk about his friend's death. He didn't want to admit what he knew was the truth, that Ciara hadn't been the reason for his death.

"Ciara was the only one you could blame. The only one you struck out at. You needed someone to blame, and she was the most convenient. Women became the scapegoat for you. Your mother abandoning you after your father left, and then in your mind Ciara taking Kyle away, a man who had become a substitute father for you."

The truth of his words pierced with arrowlike precision directly to Shane's heart.

"But it's time you did some thinking, Shane. Lay to rest a few ghosts and stop allowing the past to dictate your present, your future. A future you could have with Emma."

After Roebuck stopped speaking, the two men sat in silence. Shane became lost in thought, his mind turning over the chain of events that led him to force away the one who'd come to mean more to him than anyone in his life had, including Kyle.

"It's not too late. She hasn't left."

Shane glanced at Roebuck, his brow furrowed. "I thought she was already gone. I checked her room—"

"As soon as she got back to base, she wrapped up

and was packed, ready to go, in less than a few hours. I tried to ask her what happened after everything calmed down. She barely said a word. Just that she had what she needed for the article. She wouldn't even stay at the station, decided to stay at one of the hotels in town."

"And she's still there?" Shane asked, already rising and grabbing his jacket.

"I'm not sure about that. She just gave me her card, told me she'd be leaving as soon as she could book her flight."

Before Roebuck had completed his last sentence, Shane had his keys in hand and was running out the door.

Roebuck sat back, a satisfied smile crossing his face.

Chapter 25

The soft melody and stirring lyrics of love and loss played on the radio while Emma sat on the floor in her office, sorting through the mountain of mail that had accumulated in her absence.

She picked up an ad for a new lingerie shop opening and snorted. "Yeah, right. Doesn't look like I'll be needing any of *that* in the foreseeable future."

Balling the ad up in her fist, she tossed it into the compact trash can nearby. "She shoots, she scores!" When the wadded up piece of paper spun on the rim before tipping to the floor, she finished, "Scratch that, folks. She misses."

With a sigh, she stretched her legs out in front of her, glancing up at the clock on her desk, stretching her back.

"The story of my life," she groused.

She'd been in her office for the last three hours, reading emails, going through mail and old files badly in need of her attention…anything and everything to help keep her mind off of Shane.

Not that any of it had worked.

She glanced at the pile of mail. She had hardly made a dent. Damn.

She'd returned home two days ago, and in that time she'd cleaned every inch of her small apartment, gone through her emails and responded, spoken with her editor, and had sat down more times than she wanted to remember in an attempt to start writing the article.

But each time she sat in front of the computer, she found herself at a loss for words, her fingers lying still over the keyboard.

Something that usually came so easy to her, telling a story in article form, had painfully become the hardest task in the world. Words failed her when she needed them, her inability to write making her fear that she had nothing to say. That her gift had been taken from her. That he'd taken it from her.

Though really, she couldn't blame him.

She'd known from the first minute how he felt about her being on his turf. He had made no attempt to hide his feelings. Maybe a part of her had thought, foolishly, that she could change him. That she *had* changed him.

And for a while she thought she had succeeded. That he believed she could be trusted. She felt anger at him, as well as at herself. Why did she have to prove herself in the first place? She'd learned, often the hard way, that you could never really change anyone.

She stood up and left her small office and wandered over to stand near the balcony. Sightlessly, she stared out, her mind in turmoil.

Between his mother's desertion and eventual death and then what happened between him and Kyle, there was little room for forgiveness in Shane's life, it seemed.

And no matter how noble her intentions, he'd found her guilty of selfishness, believing she cared so little for anyone else's safety that for her article she would do just about anything. She hadn't even been allowed to explain what happened.

She had been tried and convicted without Shane even giving her the benefit of the doubt, much less an opportunity to defend herself. It was as though he had been waiting for her to screw up and prove that she couldn't be trusted. That he had wanted a reason to end their relationship.

The more she thought about it, the angrier she became. Beyond the anger, she was hurt. She'd come to care about him in ways she never thought she would—or could—for anyone.

"Who am I trying to kid? I fell 'head over heels, pick out the white dress, picket fence and two and a half kids' kind of love for the dumb jerk," she said out loud, swallowing down the lump in her throat.

It was too painful to think about.

She took a deep breath and left her balcony and headed back to her office. Pulling out her chair, she sat down and rolled herself to the desk. Her monitor flared to life as she clicked on the mouse, activating the system.

Clicking on the photo icon, seconds later a slideshow presentation began, one she'd been toying with earlier in the day. She sat back, watching the display of images cross her screen depicting her time with the smoke jumpers.

"Be gone..."

Again, the painful words he'd slung came back to haunt her.

At the time, she'd been too hurt to do much more than just sit there and take it, dumbfounded when he flung the words at her before turning and walking away.

Leaving her alone to wait for someone to bring her down had only been the second part of the insult. He'd left her alone as though he were throwing her away. As though she meant nothing to him.

Had there been a part of her that made the jump for reasons beyond helping the men? The thought entered her mind, but she shut it back out immediately. For so long she'd had to prove herself. Had to prove she was as good as everyone else for her entire life, it had felt. Had there been somewhere, buried deep in her subconscious, that her intentions, although for the right reasons, had been for the story? Had she been so desperate to prove she could write the best article that she'd go to such extreme measures to do so?

Angrily, she wiped at the tears on her face with the back of her arm. She paused, mid-sniff, looking down at her sleeve. She was wearing his T-shirt. She brought her sleeve to her nose, closed her eyes and inhaled. The shirt still carried his scent… She remembered when she'd taken the shirt. They'd just made love during the weekend they spent away from the station.

She sat up, realizing that she'd worn the T-shirt at night, every night, since the day he told her to leave.

"How pitiful am I?" She threw her hands up in disgust, shaking her head.

"Sitting here crying over someone…someone who doesn't even want me! Doesn't give a damn about me. Someone who thinks I'm so stupid…so, so…whatever the hell he thought, that I'd jump into a damn burning forest for a story!" She flung the angry words into the room before she pushed her chair away from her desk, stood, and tore his shirt from her body.

"Enough! I'm through…through, mooning over him like some teenage girl crushing over a boy."

Once removed, she balled the T-shirt up much the same way she had the newspaper ad and threw it with all her might across the room.

"He doesn't want me? Fine! Whatever! I don't need him." She continued her one-sided diatribe, her breathing heavy.

When she tore the shirt from her body, it had snagged on the necklace, the one he'd given her before he'd jumped, that she still wore around her neck.

Before she'd left, she'd stopped by his room to return it. But she hadn't been able to do it. Yes, he had been a royal ass to her, had treated her like he couldn't stand the sight of her after making love to her… Emma blew out a long breath. But in the end, she hadn't been able to give up that last link to him.

She grabbed the necklace, fumbling for the catch. Frustrated when her trembling hands wouldn't coordinate with her intent, she fisted the chain with the goal of breaking the damn thing from her neck and stopped, glancing down at it.

Opening her palm, she stared down at the old, nicked cross before bringing her arms back down to her sides. She couldn't do it, couldn't destroy something that had belonged to him. Something she knew had a lot of meaning for him, no matter how badly he'd hurt her.

She walked over and picked up his T-shirt from the floor where it had missed the trash can and carefully refolded it, her fingers caressing the soft material.

Turning, she walked into her bedroom and opened the top drawer of her dresser. Her glance raked over the items inside, a drawer in which she'd placed the few items that held meaning for her.

An old fading picture of her and her parents when she was young, her first medal for track and field, her first photojournalist award, a few keepsakes she'd gathered from her many travels…they were all things she kept and occasionally removed when she was feeling sad, lost.

With a deep sigh, she moved a few things out of the way before placing the T-shirt on top and closing the drawer.

Before closing another chapter in her life.

Chapter 26

"I'm coming, I'm coming! Hold on!"

Shane slumped against the door of Emma's apartment when he heard her yell.

He'd been knocking on her door for nearly ten minutes, after blowing up her doorbell for an additional five.

From the corner of his eye, he spied her neighbor, two doors down, peaking out from a cracked door and turned to face the woman.

"You *do* know what time it is, don't you?" she asked, a scowl on her face. Then with an indignant "Humph!" the woman spun around and went back inside her apartment, slamming the door shut.

Shortly after his arrival at the San Antonio airport, he'd contacted her editor to make sure she was still home.

Within twenty-four hours he'd left Lander on his way to find Emma. He hadn't known her address, but Roebuck had given him her editor's name and number and he'd phoned him.

He hadn't done more than identify himself before Bill had laid into him, calling Shane out as an egotistical jackass who didn't know his butt from a hole in the ground. Shane had listened, cringing at the various ways Bill explained, in minute details, just how much of a jerk he was.

Shane interrupted the conversation by saying three words. Three words had stopped her editor, mid-curse.

"I love her."

There had been a significant pause. When Bill spoke again, his voice, although still gruff, had lost some of its steam, some of its anger.

Shane had held his breath, expecting the man to give him the third degree. When he didn't, when he gave him Emma's address instead, he'd expelled the breath in one long whoosh of relief. One hurdle down.

Before ending the call, Bill had informed Shane that he had once spent six months with the military's special forces division during an in-depth story on the myriad ways a soldier could get information from an unwilling captive. And a warning of what he could and *would* do to certain parts of Shane's anatomy if he were to hurt "his girl" again. Shane had assured him he had no intention of ever hurting her again, if she were to take him back.

After touching down in Austin, he'd rented a car and driven through the late afternoon traffic toward her apartment complex.

To say he was anxious was putting it mildly. With his nerves stretched tight, Shane had driven around the large apartment complex for well over an hour, thinking and practicing out loud what he'd say to her when he saw her. Several scenarios came to mind when he thought of what her response would be when she saw him. It could go one of two ways.

Either she would allow him inside and listen patiently as he tried to explain his actions. He'd apologize for being a fool while begging her forgiveness, after which, with a tear in her eye, she would then jump into his arms and forgive him before they'd make mad passionate love.

Or…before he could open his mouth, she'd curse him out with enough gusto to make a drunken sailor on shore leave look tame.

He was hoping for the former.

He pushed away from the door when he heard movement on the other side, holding his breath when he felt her peering through the peephole.

"Emma…it's me. Shane. I'd just like to talk to you for a minute. Please."

When his pleading met silence, he continued. "I know you have every right to ignore me, to not open the door and walk away from this. I know that." He stopped, ran a frustrated hand through his hair and leaned against the door.

"But, I'm asking…begging that you don't. I'm begging you to let me in, to give me a chance to talk to you."

No way. No the hell he didn't. No way was Shane on the other side of the door, pleading for her to let him in.

No, he didn't have the utter gall to even think she'd consider it. Not after telling her to get the hell out, that he never wanted to see her again and making her feel lower than the dirt beneath his feet.

He'd told her in no uncertain terms what he thought of her, how immature she was, how self-centered. The fact that he was on her doorstep should mean nothing to her. She should walk away and let him bang at the door all night if he wanted. Let him know how it felt to be hurt, ignored and disregarded as though *he* meant nothing, as though the weeks they'd spent together meant nothing…

But instead she broke new Olympic speed records for unlatching the three locks on her door in less than two seconds.

She flung the door open, and there he stood. All six-foot-plus of hard, fine man staring down at her. She scanned his face, her hungry gaze roaming his body, her heartbeat thumping erratically against her chest, her love for him eclipsing her anger, despite her avowals to the contrary.

His facial expression was neutral, and had she not

come to know him as she had, she'd swear that he didn't care one way or another, that the pleading tone she'd heard in his voice had merely been a figment of her wishful imagination.

Her gaze was drawn to the small tic at the corner of his mouth before she met his eyes again. They were filled with enough emotion that she caught her breath in wonder. But she hardened her heart against him, remembering the pain he'd caused her when he'd thrown her away.

She crossed her arms over her body, one bare foot tapping out an angry beat against her soft carpet, ready to give completely over to the fury that strummed through her.

"*What* do you want?"

"Emma…please. Hear me out, baby."

"You can stop with the 'baby' stuff. You lost the right to call me that when you told me—hmmm—what was it you said?" she asked, scrunching her brows together in mock consideration. She snapped her fingers together. "Oh yeah, 'You're nothing more than a self-centered opportunist.'"

His face washed with a dark red stain across his cheeks.

"Would you please hear me out before you pass judgment? Please? I was wron—"

"You're damn right you were wrong!" Emma cut in, hands on her hips, warming to her anger.

"I should have listened to you when you tried to explai—"

"No!" she yelled, her temper rising with her voice

in equal measure. "Instead you chose to take the easy route and just come out blasting me, accusing me of—"

"I know. I should have listened."

They both stopped. Emma's chest rose in agitation. "Just go. I don't think I'm ready to forgive you that easily."

"Just like that, Emma?"

"Yeah. Just like that, Shane."

"I don't think so."

He advanced toward her, slamming the door behind him.

"Stop right there. Don't even think about coming any closer. If you do, I won't be accountable for my actions," she replied, throwing her hand out to ward him off, her jaw tight in anger.

When he continued to walk toward her, Emma's bravado went up in smoke. She staggered back.

As he advanced into the room, Shane's hungry eyes raked over her, starting at her coral-pink-colored toenails, past her bared, pretty brown legs and up over her breasts, her nipples stabbing against the thin fabric of the shirt she wore, until he met her gaze.

"Remember when I told you I'd laid to rest the ghosts of my past?" he asked, sitting down next to her on the sofa, close.

"Yes, I remember."

Emma glanced at him warily, uncomfortable with how close he was and the hint of his unique scent brushing across her senses. She was even more uncomfortable with the way it made her feel.

"I was telling the truth. I mean I thought I *had*. But I guess some of them were still there."

There was a short pause.

"When Kyle died, I didn't know who to blame. I was so damn mad, so hurt…so pissed off…I blamed the only person I could."

"Ciara."

"What do you…how do you know? Wait. Never mind. It was Roebuck." He answered his own question and she nodded.

He drew in a deep breath. "So you know. For a long time I blamed her. She was the reason he went into that cabin in the first place. Had she not gone inside, directly against orders, Kyle wouldn't have had to go in after her. And he'd still be alive.

"But an elderly man who owned one of the cabins begged her to try and retrieve a strongbox he kept in his bedroom that held the only mementos he had of his deceased wife, and Ciara went inside to try and get it. She cared. She really cared. She didn't think of the danger to herself. She did what many people wouldn't have. She did what Kyle would have done."

"Yet you blamed her for Kyle going inside after her?"

"She was handy." The admission was made in a low voice, one filled with shame. "But it wasn't her fault. I know that now. I think I always have."

She surprised him. "I…I can understand why you felt like that. Why you hated her for so long. At the time it seemed like she took away the one person in your life that you felt ever really cared about you. Maybe she represented for you not just women who'd disappointed you but everyone who had."

"Oh yeah, Dr. Phil, you think so?" he asked with a subtle smile.

"Well, it doesn't take a psychiatrist to see that."

"I suppose not. Just a sexy photojournalist."

Even though his quip didn't elicit a smile back from her, he breathed in a sigh of relief when he noticed her body had relaxed, losing some of its tension.

When he inched closer to her she didn't move away. Instead, conscious or not, she leaned in closer to him.

The gesture told him she still cared for him. He hoped she felt more than mere affection, prayed she felt a fraction of what he felt for her.

"Being angry at the world seemed to be my MO for a long time. My mother deserting me, Kyle's death and Ciara's involvement—it all got jumbled up in my mind, and it was just easier to keep women at a distance. It was a hell of a lot less painful that way."

"And that's why you had objections to me coming to the station?"

"It was. And it was stupid. *I* was stupid. I shouldn't have pushed you so hard, shouldn't have tried to get rid of you. And I damn sure shouldn't have accused you of grandstanding when you jumped from the plane. I was wrong. I know that now. Can you ever forgive me, Emma?" He turned with pleading eyes toward her.

Emma understood all of his reasons, even empathized

with him. But she wasn't ready to let him off the hook so quickly.

"What you said to me was painful. Not just because of the words, but because you were the first person I felt comfortable enough with to open myself up to. But at the first sign of perceived misjudgment, you threw me to the wolves, as though none of what we shared mattered. It hurt."

This time, feeling bold, he leaned over, brought her close to his body, staring down into her face, framing it with his hands.

"I know God, I know I hurt you. But please forgive me. Give me another chance, Emma. I don't want to be alone anymore. I love you."

At his halting declaration of love, Emma's heart ached, throbbed, the love she felt for him nearly suffocating her. Yes, he'd hurt her more than anyone, mostly because she loved him so much. But she needed him, too. He completed her in ways beyond the superficial. She'd never realized just how lonely she was, how much she needed someone to love, and someone who would love her just as much as she loved him.

Casting doubts to the side, she turned to face him. In her eyes he read the answer. His eyes shut briefly before he lifted her from where she stood beside him and brought her close, kissing her with an intensity that seared her flesh, branded her heart with his.

"I love you, Emma. I love you," he moaned against her mouth.

"And I love you, Shane. I love you."

Chapter 27

The light from the bedside lamp cast a golden sheen across Emma's skin, highlighting its perfection and lending her an ethereal look, belying the strength her beautiful skin clothed.

After their declaration of love, Shane had picked Emma up in his arms, and, with her guidance, led her to her bedroom.

He couldn't get enough of her.

The love she had for him shone in her dark brown eyes as he stroked inside her, their gazes locked. So much love that he briefly closed his eyes, unable to believe his good fortune. As he made love to her he mentally sent up prayers of gratitude that she had come into his life.

When a gentle smile lifted the corners of her mouth,

as though she knew his thoughts, he leaned down and placed a kiss against her lips, his hips gently swaying against hers, their lovemaking relaxed and sweet.

He groaned against her mouth, biting at her lips' perfect fullness, his need for her bordering on desperate. He couldn't get enough, couldn't get close enough.

"I love you, Shane," Emma said once again.

"Enough to marry me?"

His whispered question brought her fully awake. Emma lay beneath Shane, her body fluid, loose, completely relaxed from their lovemaking, so much so that she didn't think she would be able to move.

"What?"

"You said you loved me. Do you love me enough to marry me?" he clarified.

Emma was caught off balance, her mind still reeling from his return and their lovemaking.

"Remember when you mentioned wanting to write a book?"

She nodded, remembering when she'd casually shared her dream of taking a year off to write something more than articles. That idea had been shoved back to the corner of her mind to think about later, when she wasn't chasing a story or tearing her hair out trying to beat a deadline. In short, it was a dream.

"Yes, but what has that got—"

He kissed her, cutting off her words.

"Hear me out."

She laughed lightly. "Okay. I'm all ears."

"As you know, there aren't many full-time jumpers. I'm one of a few of them."

"Yes…"

"Sometimes I travel, jump fires everywhere. I've even jumped them outside the U.S."

"Okay…"

"What would you think about writing a fictional book about that? I don't know, you could place the story anywhere. It doesn't even have to be about jumpers. Although it would be hot as hell. Pun intended," he said, wiggling his eyebrows. Emma groaned and then laughed along with him at his lame joke.

"Seriously, Emma," he said, once their laughter subsided.

"I don't know, Shane." She shrugged one shoulder. "I don't know if that's what I want."

"You don't know if you want to write the book…or you don't know if you want me?" he asked, his face tightening.

He moved away far enough to see her face. Reaching out, he placed both of his hands on either side of her and she closed her eyes, unable to cope with the raw emotion, the hope and fear reflected in them.

"No! Open your eyes. Look at me."

She did, swallowing down the tears burning her throat.

"I love you. More than I thought I could ever love anyone. I probably don't deserve you." He leaned in and kissed her on the lips. "But if you give me a chance I promise I won't hurt you. I'll never reject you again. I'll spend the rest of my life making sure you never feel alone again, make sure you never feel nothing but love."

"Shane, I don't know. Is this what you want? Really?" she asked, a small catch in her voice, tears burning the corners of her eyes. "Is this what *I* want? Or are we two people who are so used to being alone, emotionally, that we can't—"

"Don't say it. Emma, please…" He stopped, drawing in a breath.

He gathered her back into his arms. "All I know is that I never knew what real happiness was until you came into my life. I never knew what real love was. When you left, I realized how empty my life would be without you in it." His voice broke. Clearing his throat, he continued. "I love you. I love everything about you. Even those weird little pig-sounding snores you make in your sleep," he said, and she punched him lightly, giggling softly past the tears choking her.

"I love everything about you, Emma. We can work on everything else. Hell, if you want to keep doing photojournalism and traveling, I'll give up jumping."

"Shane!"

"I'm serious, Emma. I'd follow you to the ends of the earth if it means we'll be together."

He claimed her lips with his. Turning her body, he placed her beneath him, not releasing her mouth.

Emma, one who was rarely at a loss for words, found herself unable to speak, her mind in a chaotic whirl.

Her eyes searched his, for something, anything, to help her as she considered his request. What she saw, what came shining brightly through, was honesty… and love.

And she loved him just as much as he loved her. Loved him from the first time she'd seen him scowling at her. Loved him with everything she had.

Their time together had been short, but Emma felt as though she'd known him for a thousand lifetimes, in that place that defied logic. That place that told her their love would last a lifetime. In that place that whispered to her to jump now, grab him and don't let go.

She had no intention of letting him go.

A smile began to blossom on his face as he read her response. With a shout, he grabbed her and hugged her as though he would never let her go. Emma clung to him as he showered her face with his kisses.

"Yes, I'll marry you," she answered, laughing happily. And although he already knew, the smile on his handsome face grew brighter when he drew away from her.

"I will never let you down, again, baby. I promise you. I'll always be there for you."

When he tried to bring her back into his arms, she pushed back, holding him at bay, one side of her lips quirking.

"Even if I decide to jump into another fire?"

He barked out a laugh. "Only if I'm jumping right there beside you!"

* * * * *

Wilde IN **WYOMING** *Saddle Up...to a Wilde*

Kimberly Kaye Terry

*invites you to discover
the Wilde brothers of Wyoming*

Book #1
TO TEMPT A WILDE
On Sale February 22, 2011

Book #2
TO LOVE A WILDE
On Sale March 29, 2011

Book #3
TO DESIRE A WILDE
On Sale April 26, 2011

www.kimanipress.com

KPWIWSP

REQUEST YOUR FREE BOOKS!

2 FREE NOVELS
PLUS 2 FREE GIFTS!

KIMANI™ ROMANCE

Love's ultimate destination!

A DANGEROUS LINE LIES BETWEEN
PASSION AND LOYALTY, DUTY AND DESIRE....

ESSENCE BESTSELLING AUTHOR

DONNA HILL

Dynamic activist
Samantha Montgomery
faces the controversy of a
lifetime when she agrees to
help handsome civil rights
attorney Chad Rushmore
take on a landmark police-
brutality case. Not only
does their sudden, fiery
attraction endanger the
already troubled lawsuit,
but it puts Samantha at
heartbreaking odds with
her attorney sister!

A SCANDALOUS AFFAIR

"Superb writing, a riveting plot, real characters and a definite
but not preachy stance on a topic that is touchy at best makes
this an excellent book."
—*RT Book Reviews* on *A SCANDALOUS AFFAIR*

*Coming the first week of December 2010
wherever books are sold.*

ARABESQUE®

www.kimanipress.com

KPDH1921210